Matt,

Your writing is awesq[...]
enjoyable. Thanks for he[...]   as
Publishers Come true.

—Long Shot Books

Atomic Flyswatter Vol. I

We would like to thank the writers included in this long awaited anthology for their patience and for their contributions that have made it well worth the wait.

We also thank Taylor Pannell for her awesome cover art.

Table of Contents

A Phone Booth, Far Away
By Alexandre Ferrere

The Bell struck noon,
     each
     note
     crawling under the deserted Chirico sun
& he got kissed behind the church
& woke up at dawn,

          (beauty of bodies spreading in white space,
           beauty in muscles arms legs floating,
            beauty in bubbles of steam,
       beauty over boiling secret bursting into History)

thirsty,
& reifying unanswered prayers
through yesterday's eyes. "Cars
     are going too fast", he said ("O, the rhythm
        box by the sea", he thought),
   "so many extra ordinary flowers
   so many
   so many that they're pushed
     towards the usual.
   I miss one phone
     booth
   which rang for no
       thing
      for no
        body ("though I've never used one" he thought).

A dream of virgin islands
      of savage landscapes
naked, afraid of tigers for real

       but had to slow
        & stop:
       " the red light is hurting my eyes
       & thoughts" he said
       or thought/

The amount of flesh & space uncoiling
in the rear view is nothing
compared to the ghosts of time endlessly howling in the void,
unheard, blatant,
lost
in the blind spot of memory.
      "Do you remember the time when...
      "where" would be more accurate"
          he said
           or thought
             or whatever.

Stuck Pages in a Forgotten Diary
By Alexandre Ferrere

Be
fore thoughts, that
is Time with
out seasons, there
was no truth in me
mories. Re
member the eve
nings with clouds
so dense we danced & play
ed at finding forms with   holes like
negatives of a moonlit   sky   We did
not own one night   but   all of them   at/for once.

Later I play
ed the blues to an absent
crowd &
there it was: it.

Echoes of images
now in my mind
fall like rain.

Skeleton Wings
By Alyssa Cooper

When she sits in the garden,
I can see the sun glinting in her wings, as they flutter above her back.
She presses her thumbs into the bruises on her thighs,
and she smiles without her eyes,
    without teeth,
and the tendons in her arms ripple like violin strings.

I could play music in the crease of her elbow.

She weaves a crown of roses with her skeleton fingers,
and she wears it over her wild-forest-fairy hair,
and the thorns rest against her marble skin, but they don't draw blood,
and I wonder if she is made of stone,
    I wonder if her veins are empty,
and she can hear my thoughts.

I can tell, in the way that she averts her eyes.

Even when darkness falls,
when the rains come,
when winter snow dusts her shoulders like an ermine stole,
she refuses my invitation to come inside;
I leave the doors open while I sleep,
    letting in the wind and night,
and she weaves her crowns in the garden.

She fixes her eyes on the horizon.

She flutters her wings.

And she waits

Koschei and Marya
By Alyssa Cooper

Let me sit at your feet like a dog.

It is hard to explain
how I want you to choose my food,
and feed me from your own spoon,
how I want you to stroke my hair
and pull my head onto your knee, how

in my mind,

I call you master;
hard to explain how I tried for ten years
to find some sense of control,
and yet when you arrived,
you handed it over with no more ceremony
than if it were a scrap of dried liver from

your pocket.

With a single command,
you undid a decade of doing,
like magic,
like a stubborn puppy,
finally learning to sit,
on the fifteenth try.

So let me kneel at your feet,
with my smooth new flesh and
my absolved hands.
Pull my head onto your knee,
and feed me from your fingertips.
Give me new commands,
and I will try to learn.

Teach me to speak.
Teach me to rest.

Teach me to stay.

Storming Mind
By Amanda Suder

Wishing, wanting, asking, yearning.	"You wish, you want, you ask, you yearn.
Water cooling, fire burning.	I'm the fire in which you burn.
Ache inside and ache on skin.	You ache inside you ache on skin.
Never show the storm within.	I can quell the storm within.
Always rushing, never slowing.	Always rushing, never slowing.
Floods of water just keep flowing.	Floods of water I can stop flowing.
Thunder crashes, lightning shines.	Thunder crashes, lightning shines.
Portrait of a troubled mind.	I can calm your troubled mind.
She is calling, begging, pleading.	You are calling, begging, pleading.
Wanting freedom never seeing.	I am answering. I am seeing.
Lost inside her own dark head.	Lost inside your own dark head.
Wishing she could go to bed.	Let my voice inside you spread."

Ruins
By Amanda Suder

Quick and easy, short not long,

time is fleeting, like a song.

Even echoes pass away.

Night has come. Goodbye day.

Empty shadows cover walls.

As they fill the crumbling halls.

Passing through this shattered place,

everyone's gone. I've lost the race.

Quiet whispers, quickened steps,

stumbling through what has been left.

Like a ghost of long passed age,

I too will soon simply fade away.

Nothing anchors. Nothing holds.

Darkness pulls me to its folds.

I fall. I sink. I soar. I fly,

as my life passes me by.

Then a hand reaches down,

and pulls me from the darkened ground.

It brings me close and holds me tight.

A voice says "everything will be alright."

The Sweet Spot
By Andy Valentine

Dirtbag hated baseball. You could tell from his body. He was a scaly blonde lemon-shaped boy with pippy teeth and overlong gums. Of course, the lemon association was compounded by his *being* an absolute lemon. Lemon on base, lemon at bat, lemon way out far left-field. To say he sucked is putting it kindly. He looked awkward out there, wrist swelling over his mitt, jersey stuck to his gut like cling wrap. Off the field he favored Kirkland jeans with elastic waistbands, flat-footed shoes and cotton shirts. His collection of band tees was one for the books. The first thing he ever asked me was, "Do you like Nirvana?"

His real name was Toby Wheatus-Longe. We called him Dirtbag because of the song, "Teenage Dirtbag." The song itself had no edge, and for this reason he despised it. His hatred for whiny music even outweighed his distaste for baseball. But nicknames stick, and in my mind Dirtbag will always be Dirtbag. Better than Lemon, I always thought.

Then there was Dirtbag's dad. He was the guy you always saw with his nose pressed on the dugout fence, yelling clichés like "Good eye," "Let's hear some chatter" and "Hey batter batter sah-*wing!*"

Practice was held on Tuesdays and Thursdays, and games were played each Friday night. It wasn't a real competitive league. It wasn't really a league at all. It was club baseball. There were no try-outs. The roster was created in an office somewhere, from names printed on registration forms. No one dreamed of going pro, of moving on to play in college. No one thought they were the next Babe Ruth or Edgar Martinez. We were there to appease our parents.

Thirteen is a funny age because parents start to glom on tight. They've led you up to this imaginary door and you're ready to go, to step outside. But all of a sudden they grab your arm and try their best to pull you back. So you wind up playing baseball. Now your parents have something to root for.

Dirtbag's dad was the team's de facto mascot. He took us for pizza after the games. While we ate, he lectured us about our mistakes. Dirtbag's face would redden slowly as his dad sipped beer and said things like, "We need to keep those bases tight," or "Too many holes in the outfield wall."

There was a sadness about him, Dirtbag's dad. You had to look close if you wanted to see it, but it was there, buried beneath the whites of his eyes and the whiskered lines around his mouth.

One time I saw him cry. It was July 4th. Me and some of the guys were over at Dirtbag's house for a team barbecue. All the parents were in the back yard, drinking Aperol spritz and standing around while the hotdogs cooked. Through the window I could hear my dad. He was talking to Dirtbag's mom about something, using that voice he always used when my mom was ill. A kind of steady, caring lilt like he was trying to coax the sickness from her. Dirtbag had his blinds closed. His bedroom was humid with all of us in there, sitting sideways across his bed.

We were watching *Reservoir Dogs*. Dirtbag kept pausing the film and pointing to things (like orange jars in the back of a shot) and explaining their significance. He said the jars were a form of foreshadowing because it turned out Mr. Orange was a rat all along. Most of the guys left after that, muttering about how the movie was ruined. Scott Mitty and Johnny Drake stayed behind with Dirtbag and me. We watched the film a while longer, growing quiet when Mr. Blonde pulled his razor.

"Stealers Wheel," Dirtbag laughed. "What a joke."

I didn't like the song much, either. But unlike Dirtbag, who disliked it for purely musical reasons, I was never able to detach the words "Stuck in the middle with you" from the sight of that bloody ear-stump. When the scene was over my stomach felt sour. I could tell by the look on Johnny's face that he was feeling queasy too.

"Hey," I said, finding any excuse for a break. "You wanna see something cool?"

I ran down to the yard and located my parents. They were milling around in separate corners. My dad was still talking to Dirtbag's mom. As I approached, she stopped mid-sentence and gazed at her wine.

"What's going on?" my dad said.

"Can I have the car keys? I want to get my roman candles."

My dad glanced at Mrs. Wheatus-Longe, who returned a faint, nervous smile.

I jogged around to the cul-de-sac and opened the trunk of my dad's RAV4. The car was old, but dad kept a stockpile of those pine-tree air fresheners in the center console. The blue ones branded, "New Car Smell." As I raised the liftgate a false, heavy stink drifted out of the trunk. It reminded me of gasoline, and I felt sick again, picturing Mr. Blonde with a lighter.

Dirtbag and Scott were alone in the bedroom. Johnny Drake had gone downstairs. The movie was paused and they were flipping through an issue of *Rolling Stone*. Dirtbag turned the page and said, "Tom Morello's a riff ma*chine*."

Scott stopped reading and gave me a look. "So what's this cool thing?"

"Check it out," I reached into the plastic bag and produced one of the roman candles.

Dirtbag grinned. "Out front, right now."

When a roman candle fires it makes a short whooshing sound like pinched air escaping a plug. The flare arcs toward the target, trembling and bright, and lands with a tiny, sizzling breath. It doesn't hurt when the firework hits you—more so stings, like a horsefly bite. You might end up with an itchy welt, or find a hole in your T-shirt later. That's how most roman candle fights go. But Dirtbag, he was in the zone. I must have been hit fifteen times. Scott, too. We both got it bad. If you dodged to one side, the flare seemed to follow as though caught in a slip-stream. Dirtbag had this fire in his eyes.

When my candle died I sprinted onto Dirtbag's lawn and hid in the bushes beneath the front window. Looking out, catching my breath, I saw Scott take cover behind my dad's car. Dirtbag stood at the cul-de-sac's center, firing upward into the sky, the colored flames splitting and falling. He tipped his head and roared—this deep, manly otherworld roar—and I felt a jolt inside my chest; a sinister feeling of things turned bad, of a game becoming more than a game.

The fireworks stopped and Dirtbag let his arm go slack. I crouched silently, raking my fingertips over the soil. Scott emerged checking his clothes. I turned to the house and studied my reflection in the window. My cheeks were flushed. A lacquer of sweat shined on my forehead. As my eyes refocused I realized I was looking into Dirtbag's living room. My heart bounced. Dirtbag's dad was sitting inside, faced diagonally away from the window. There were streaks of moisture below his eye, the one nearest me. He was holding a drink, the liquid trembling, ice shifting. His whole body was shaking. He rocked forward and cupped his face with his opposite hand. Then, as though sensing my presence, he turned and stared directly at me. His eyes were crushed, webbed with vessels. We looked at each other for an endless second. Then I was up, stumbling backwards, turning and hurrying back to the street.

We ate hotdogs and drank Shasta and people-watched each other's parents. Michael Green's stepmom was 20 years old. She looked like a kid, hand in hand with Mr. Green. We all agreed we'd like to finger her. In the far back corner, my mom had joined Mrs. Wheatus-Longe and my dad. They were all three sort of drunk. I could tell because their cheeks were blotchy, the way people look at Thanksgiving dinner. They seemed to be talking very intently. My parents were leaning toward Dirtbag's mom, and she was leaning in to them. Dirtbag's dad was still inside. I hadn't said a word about it.

As the sun went down, all the life drained out of the sky. Lingering smells of firework smoke, canned beer and kosher franks. In the distance, mortars screamed and you could see the tips of their blossoming bursts long before you heard them blow. The crowd thinned out slowly at first, then I blinked and it was Dirtbag and me, alone in the yard with his mom and my parents. They were still talking, off in their corner. My mom and dad held their glasses in opposite hands, and the hands between them were nearly touching, hesitating, as though waiting for something to fill the gap.

"I know what they're talking about," Dirtbag said.

The grown-ups were suddenly there beside us. Mrs. Wheatus-Longe stepped onto the deck and disappeared through the sliding door. Dirtbag stood and followed her in. I looked at my parents. Dad's head appeared to be troubling him. It kept falling forwards, or sideways, or tilting back, like a basketball balanced on top of a stick. My mom leaned in and kissed my hair.

"Marcy—Mrs. Wheatus-Longe—is staying at our house tonight," she said. She smelled of water and halos and wine. "How'd you like to sleep here? You can have a sleepover with your little friend Toby."

"What's going on?" I said. "I don't want to stay here."

"Toby's dad will take care of you," she said. "And we'll come pick you up in the morning."

"But—"

"It's okay," dad said. "It's okay." He sniffed and blinked, sniffed and blinked. His neck shivered.

"Can't you just tell me what happened?"

Mom shrugged. "It's grown-up stuff."

A firework exploded somewhere nearby. We all looked skyward, searching for colors. The sliding door hissed and Dirtbag's mom came out of the house with a look on her face like she'd let something go. A duffel bag hung from the nape of her elbow.

"Ready?" she asked, and my parents nodded. Mom squeezed my shoulder and followed my dad, trailing Mrs. Wheatus-Longe, through the side gate and out of sight. I sat in the gathering darkness and listened to the RAV4 fade away.

Dirtbag's dad had the TV going. The living room smelled of beer potpourri. He threw a double-take as I paused on my way to the stairs.

"Mariners Giants," he said, nodding at the screen. He tipped his drink and belched. "1995."

It seemed useless to stand there avoiding his eyes. I climbed the stairs. Dirtbag was finishing *Reservoir Dogs*. He was slumped on the bed, face blue by the light of the screen. It was like walking into a mirror image of the scene I'd just left, only younger, stormier. It struck me that there were two parts of the same house being used in identical ways, while other rooms sat in mismatched darkness. You could feel your breath drifting away and pooling in those empty rooms.

I sat beside Dirtbag and allowed my eyes to well out of focus. There was a prickling sensation on the back of my neck. Finally I turned to Dirtbag and asked the question I was dying to ask.

"What did you mean?" I said. "Before, when you said you knew what they were talking about."

Dirtbag said nothing. It was the closing shot. Harvey Keitel was covered in blood and holding a gun to Tim Roth's head.

In the night a falling sensation woke me. I sat up. The carpet beneath me was damp. Through the window I heard a crackle and realized the fireworks were still going off. My heart rushed inside my ears. I lay back down and tried to sleep, but persistent pops and explosions stopped me. In the distance, I thought I heard laughter. Then it came closer. My eyelids cracked as a rocket flashed, filling the room with brilliant light. Dirtbag's dad stood in the doorway. He looked like fucking Nosferatu. I shut my eyes.

"Hey, kid," I heard him say. "Can't sleep?" I lay there paralyzed. A floorboard creaked under the carpet. "Come on," he said. "I'm watching the game."

When I opened my eyes, the room was dark. "You scared me," I said.

"Just come downstairs."

As I followed him down, a lump of dread grew in my chest. I didn't know what was going to happen. In my mind, I kept replaying the moment we'd shared. I'd caught him in a place of weakness, of humiliation, and now maybe he wanted revenge. Maybe he was going to spank me. I imagined myself bare-assed over his lap, his hand striking again and again.

"Look who's crying now, *spy!*"

A lamp shined dully inside the living room. Bottles and cans and empty glasses covered the coffee table. The window was open and the air from outside was perfumed with gunpowder.

"Sit down there," he said, pointing to the couch. I sidled past him, aware of his gaze, and sank quietly onto the cushion. The moment was coming. I could feel it in the silence, that gap between launch and exquisite kaboom. Even as I watched him rewind the tape, settle back in the chair by the window, push play and crack a beer, I felt the room shrink like the pressurized tract of an aerosol can.

The picture was twitchy at first. Lines of static sectioned the screen while the VCR tracked. When the tape caught up things clicked into focus. The Mariners Giants game, 1995. I looked at Dirtbag's dad, wondering why he'd brought me down here if not to spank me or hurt me somehow. Was there torture in watching an outdated ballgame? Broadcast baseball was boring at times, but it wasn't all that hard to sit through. Televised golf, *there* was punishment.

But a coldness extended from the place where he sat that made my hair stand on end. He was watching closely, too closely, as though trying to spot a flaw in the tape or find something minuscule lost in the grass. As a pitch fired off and the hitter swung, sending the ball out into the crowd, Dirtbag's dad leaned so far forward that the armchair's rear legs rose from the carpet.

"There!" he hissed. "There! There!"

He fumbled with the buttons on the remote, paused the tape, rewound several fuzzy frames and stopped again on a shot of the crowd.

"Do you see us?" he said, his excitement growing. "There we are!"

You had to squint in order to see it, but there they were, no doubt about it. The Wheatus-Longe family, cheering and smiling among the stands. Five-year-old Dirtbag in an oversized M's cap, face bright beneath the bill. Dirtbag's mom, young and festive and happy and tight, her hair permed in a dense blonde crest. And there in the middle with eyes turned up was Dirtbag's dad.

He looked ecstatic, frozen in time. But the face of the man in the frame before me did not reflect the face in the room. With a burst of movement, Dirtbag's dad hurled the beer can over his shoulder and fell to the floor. He crawled to the TV and pressed his cheek against the screen. He kissed and licked and stroked the image, babbling wetly.

"Open," he said. "Open, open. Jesus, Marcy! I hate that word."

From the choking sound that followed, you would have thought he'd been punched in the throat.

"What are you doing?" A voice from the doorway made me flinch. Dirtbag entered in his underwear, cellulite churning, slick with sweat. He had stretch marks on his belly. "What the hell, dad. Mom said you weren't allowed to watch this anymore."

Dirtbag's dad shuddered. He looked frail, broken as he knelt on the carpet. In the space between his nose and mouth, a lather of snot and spittle had formed. He looked at his son with chlorine eyes, the ones I'd seen that same afternoon, and let himself collapse into tears.

My parents couldn't come quickly enough. I wanted to dive through the window Dukes of Hazzard style and tell my dad to drive forever. As the house grew small and we turned a corner, I craned my neck for one last look. There was a creature dwelling inside that home. The kind you sense when you can't fall asleep, breathing somewhere out in the darkness, that disappears when the sun comes up.

Dirtbag's mom was still at our house. She was in the kitchen, drinking coffee from a Best Mom Ever mug. All the time we'd owned that mug, I'd only seen it tell the truth. My mom would blow across her tea, close her eyes and smile, allowing the steam to wet her face. She was truly the best mom ever. But this woman here, with her plaid pajamas and wire-brush hair, she was something entirely *less*. At least in my kitchen, perched on the stool where my mom always sat.

She stayed for a week and a half, and never once left the house. Her beauty products cluttered the bathroom. A wad of her hair plugged the tub and it didn't drain for a day and a half. In the end my dad brought out his snake and fixed the clog with a ton of cuss words. Most days he seemed put out by her presence. My mom, too, appeared impatient. But when nighttime came, everything changed. I could hear them all through the floor of my bedroom, drinking wine and laughing together. The laughter would rise to a strange, mature head and soften into a soothing drawl. Then it went silent.

I don't know where she slept each night, but it wasn't downstairs and it wasn't in the guest-room.

Two days after she left, we played a team from Wilsonville. Apparently they were the only team in our league that took baseball seriously. The kids were like towers of pubescent muscle. Even before the first inning started, we could tell they were going to tan our hides. The ball whistled from player to player, hitting each mitt with a resonant smack. Their practicing hitter looked like a mountain. His stance was triangular he got so low, and when he swung you could hear the air parting in fear.

Through the chain-link behind home base, the bleachers were packed with yammering parents, everyone dressed in loose, flowing clothes. Dirtbag's dad stood near the fence, his long fingers laced through the wire, watching our movements. Mrs. Wheatus-Longe sat in the first row, two yards behind her husband, face gray in the shade of her sunhat. The umpire gestured for the first inning to start. A round of applause rose from the bleachers.

I was at shortstop and Johnny Drake stood on the pitcher's mound. We conferred briefly about how hard this was going to suck. To the parents, it must have looked like we had a plan. But it was only a way to buy some time before the inevitable creaming began.

And creamed we were. On the very first hit they learned our weakness, when the ball careened into far left-field and Dirtbag let it roll through his legs. Every hit from there on out seemed to gravitate toward Dirtbag's corner. I kept looking at Dirtbag's dad, expecting to find him blue in the face. But with each missed scoop and ill-placed throw from his son's position, the man simply looked on in silence.

It's a law of nature that fibers snap if they're stretched too thin. This snap occurred at the top of the fourth. Johnny Drake pitched a neat little curve and the hitter hooked it high and wide. You could see it coming a mile away. Even Dirtbag with all his weight had time to position himself under the ball. He raised his arm, mitt outstretched, and a deafening silence came over the field. Empires rose and fell in that moment. The ball spiraled, hit his glove like a stone on concrete, bounced back and fell to the grass. Even the hitter stopped his dash to make sure it really happened. Dirtbag's face seemed to blister and boil, flaring a cardinal shade of red.

The field was quiet. Then a cry, an inhuman screech, broke out behind me. Dirtbag's dad was shaking the chain-link, cursing and screaming, hands clenched, eyes wide. The fence shook from bottom to top.

"No!" he yelled. "That wasn't real! You worthless piece of fucking—"

He was cut short by his wife, who'd leapt from her seat and begun to attack his scalp with her sunhat. The other parents began to murmur. I stood at shortstop, glued to the scene. Dirtbag's dad looked stunned for a moment. Then the torrent of screams continued. He gripped the fence like a captive ape, baring his teeth and shouting cuss words. The sunhat clapped against his back, over and over; a desperate attempt to shut him up. But he kept going, kicking and spitting and throwing insults toward his son. Eventually he turned to his wife, who by now had rolled the sunhat up like a newspaper and was really giving it all she had.

"You bitch!" he said, dodging her blows. "*You* made this happen! It's your fault it came to this!"

Dirtbag's mom dropped the hat. You could almost hear her knuckles pop as her fist collided with his chin. He went down cold. A collective gasp rose from the bleachers. Then three guys descended the steps, my dad among them, and carried Dirtbag's dad away. Mrs Wheatus-Longe followed them off, hiding her eyes from the murmuring crowd.

After that the game was ruined. The other team became awkward and grim. You could tell we all just wanted to leave. The ninth inning crept up slowly, and at last we came to the final play. Somebody groaned. The dugout bench had been exhausted, all except our lemon boy. I watched him squeeze his helmet on. Then he walked toward the plate. The mountain kid yelled, "Easy out!" and all the outfielders took a step in.

Maybe I didn't quite grasp the rift that tore Dirtbag's folks apart. But somewhere in the back of my mind, I knew Dirtbag knew. He'd told me so on the Fourth of July. So the look on his face as the pitch went out made perfect sense, at least to me. He was sending their problems—whatever they were—over that fence at the edge of the park.

When the ball was in range, Dirtbag swung. With the sunset behind him he looked like a shadow, a darkened mass of potential energy. His bat whisked the air and struck the ball right in the sweet spot: *Crack!* The cleanest sound I ever heard. As Dirtbag jogged, red-faced and winded, back to home, the bleachers erupted with whistles and shouts. Shoes drummed the aluminum steps, sending waves of metallic applause echoing over the field of play and out across the grass beyond. You could hear the chain-link rattle and sway, all our parents cheered so loud. And I'm sure Dirtbag's parents might have cheered too—that shot could have carried them back through time, to a certain frame on an overwatched tape—if only they'd been there to see it.

Preserving the Grounds
By Bryan Jones

Tom Hutchinson had received a call that one of his company trucks had been in an accident. The morning temperature in the Houston area was already in the nineties. The area outside the city limits still had farms. Barbed wire marked the perimeters of the pastures. Tom made record time getting out to the scene. He was the first one to arrive. When he walked up to the wreckage, he tried to estimate the truck's speed when it had veered off the road and struck the massive oak tree that was now providing the only shade on the roadside. It was a single-vehicle accident. Inside the twisted metal of the cab, his brother-in-law's lifeless body lay pinned. Tom pulled out his cell phone and called his sister. He told Linda what had happened. He said he was on his way to her place and he ended the call.

Tom was forty-two. Steve had worked for Tom's company for the last four years. They provided real estate appraisal services. Commercial and residential. Many of Tom's employees had to travel and the company owned three trucks, including the one that was now crumpled at the base of the oak tree's trunk. Tom returned his cell phone to his pocket and he stared at the demolished vehicle showered in broken windshield glass and oak leaves. He knew he needed to keep his head together for Linda's sake. He walked around to the passenger-side door. He couldn't look at Steve's body, or the blood. Nearly everything was crushed and shattered inside the cab. But when Tom stared down through the jagged hole that had once been the passenger-side window, he saw a notepad lying on the seat and recognized Steve's handwriting on the white paper. Tom reached inside and removed the notepad from the truck.

Suddenly, another car pulled off the road and came to a stop. Tom concealed the notepad from the view of the driver. Tom stepped away from the truck. The man in the car had a cell phone to his ear. Tom went back to his car and put the notepad in the trunk. A few minutes later, the driver got out of his car. The man's dress shirt and slacks did not suggest that he was part of an emergency response team or that he had any other official reason to be there.

"I called 911," the man said. "Is the driver dead?"

Tom looked down and nodded. He decided not to tell the man his company owned the truck. In the distance, Tom could hear the approaching sirens of police and emergency vehicles. The man walked over to the wreckage. Tom went back to his car and opened the door. He got behind the wheel. For a moment, he watched through the windshield as the man circled the destroyed truck. Tom started his engine and pulled out onto the road.

Tom's cell phone rang when he hit the traffic on the Loop. It was Linda. She was distraught. She was with Steve's parents. She had her four-year-old daughter, Karen, with her. She needed him. He was her older brother. Tom said he'd be there soon. Then he ended the call. He had to hurry, but on his way, his indecision gave rise to something like an impulse, and he turned off when he saw a sign for one of the city parks on the bayou.

Tom traveled down a narrow street through an older neighborhood until he found the park entrance. He found the designated lot and pulled to a stop. He got out of his car, took off his suit jacket, and threw it on the back seat. He looked down at his rumpled slacks and shirt, his scuffed shoes. He had worn his suit that morning for a meeting he'd have to cancel. He walked around to the trunk and opened it. He took out the white notepad and read the note again.

Oak trees shaded the little stretch of park property. Heavy clumps of Spanish moss hung from tree limbs and invisible cicadas whirred from behind the leaves. There were wooden benches and picnic tables. Tom took the notepad and left his car to follow a trail bordered by flat white stones leading down to the bayou.

As he walked down the trail, his mind raced ahead to thoughts of Linda and her little girl. Suddenly, Tom felt unprepared to help his sister. He had been there for his sister when Steve had needed a job. He had always tried to protect his sister. He remembered something from when he and Linda were kids. They had played in their kitchen, making cellophane parachutes for plastic army men. They had used kite string and tape to make them. Then they had gone out into the street and cocked their arms back to throw the army men high into the air. The little parachutes had opened fast, and twirled, before they had fallen slowly back to the asphalt street. Tom remembered Linda when she was seven years old reaching down to pick up those cellophane parachutes. He remembered watching out for cars coming down the street. That was before his father's heart attack. Before Tom had become the man of the family. He had learned to be protective.

The trail divided near the banks of the bayou. Tom stopped walking and looked down at the odd patches of sand and thick weeds next to the water. The bayou moved slowly today, nothing like when he had seen it churning at flood stage, the water raging, pushing trash and debris downstream. Large trees lined the banks. Here and there, remnants from the last flood were caught in some of the drooping branches overhanging the water. A car tire was lodged between some tree roots. Next to it, a child's discarded tee shirt caught on a limb waved like a flag. Thirty yards across the width of the bayou, Tom stared at the red clay and sand of the opposite bank that had been ravaged by the effects of erosion.

Back on his bank, to the right, Tom noticed a park-maintenance man walking along the trail between the trees. Even at a distance Tom could see the man's drab uniform and baseball cap and work boots. Tom watched the man stabbing pieces of trash with a spiked stick, lifting the little pieces of newspaper and Styrofoam out of the grass so he could pluck them off the spike and put them in a plastic garbage bag attached to his waist. It looked like hot, uncomfortable work.

Points of light on the green water caught Tom's eye and he remembered after his divorce when he got the news that his little sister was getting married. Linda's face had glowed on her wedding day when he had given her away. His memories of Steve that day were vague, but Tom remembered clearly how the white wax columns of the church candles had melted down through the service. When the big question was asked, Tom had held his breath with the rest of the audience until the answers came. Then, with a chorus of sighs, his little sister had been married. At the reception, white and silver balloons had hung like strings of giant pearls at the reception. Later, discarded white paper napkins on the scuffed floor had looked like fallen leaves.

She had never lived far from Tom. After Tom's divorce, he had moved into a house that was only twenty minutes away from where Steve and Linda lived. Steve had only been able to afford that house because of the job Tom had given him. They invited each other over to watch football and basketball games. Linda had wanted Steve and Tom to be friends.

Off to the left, Tom could see where the bayou widened between high banks that were spanned by a large, seemingly indestructible bridge. There were ripples around some of the massive concrete piers that had been sunk deep into the mud and sand in order to support the structure. To even think of the bridge failing during rush-hour was to imagine a catastrophic death toll.

Not long after Tom had hired Steve, the two men had taken a short flight to meet with employees from the state environmental agency who had found some diesel fuel contamination on one of the properties a client was considering purchasing. Steve had never flown before. It had been hard to focus Steve on company matters after the airplane pulled up to the gate. Tom had noticed how Steve kept rotating the wedding ring on his finger as he spoke in nervous bursts about how his parents had always chosen to drive on their summer vacations. Some of those vacations had involved riding for a week in the family station wagon as his parents took turns driving them all up to Vermont where his father had been born. Steve had tried to describe to Tom these childhood memories as the two men sat in the uncomfortable airport chairs surrounded by all the usual distractions of loud conversations, crackling announcements over the loudspeakers, and someone with a persistent and troubling cough. Everyone hoped that man with the cough had been booked on someone else's flight. Then a small child had run past them, spinning the plastic propellers of his toy airplane, making the bomber bank right, and then left, until he dropped to his knees and nose-dived the plane into the blue carpet. The boy's fat lips made an explosion sound. Steve had been very quiet after that. It hadn't been until after they had touched down two hours later and swallowed a couple of stiff drinks in the airport bar that Steve had managed to laugh about his first flight.

Tom couldn't understand Steve's decision to multiply it all by zero. Had there been too much pressure on Steve at work? Tom rejected the thought. The workloads and schedules had been manageable. Tom refused to take any blame and wouldn't tolerate any guilt over what Steve had done. Guilt implied responsibility and Tom wasn't responsible for something he couldn't control. Tom checked his cell phone and saw there'd been a call from his insurance company. He knew he'd have to return the call. They had questions. The investigation would go on for some time. They'd ask about Steve's depression. Tom didn't know what he would tell them. He remembered Linda mentioning something about medication that had made Steve drowsy at times. Steve had said he didn't like to talk about it, and Tom had always sensed that Steve felt it was a weakness, something that a strong person should be able to overcome through sheer will.

But now there'd be an investigation. Tom stood at the bayou's edge and thought about Linda and Karen. He didn't know how his sister would survive this. Tom looked at the writing on the notepad, the anguished ballpoint scrawl, words that made no sense. Tom thought about all the eyes that would pore over the words. Tom wondered if the note had been written long before the crash, but very few clues were evident. There were only weak and broken words written on the page, an ugly kind of despair that Tom wanted to turn away from. It was exactly what Tom had always imagined such notes would sound like, strings of sentences that failed to explain, to justify, to excuse. Linda would want answers. When she got older, Karen would want answers, too. But there weren't any answers in the note. All he had were two pages of evidence showing Steve had deliberately veered off the road. More than anything, Tom felt the need to protect Linda and Karen from what the note proved. Tom wanted to give them at least the possibility that it had been an accident. It would be easier to understand this as the tragic consequence of Steve having fallen asleep behind the wheel of a moving vehicle. In one part of the note, Steve blamed Linda for his pain. Tom didn't want his sister to have to read these words that would leave their own particular scars on every memory of her marriage. He wanted to shield her from knowing this, but this was what Steve had wanted to leave behind for Linda and Karen. The note was meant for them. Tom didn't know if he had the right to substitute a permanent silence for a devastating truth.

Tom made his decision. He ripped the first page from the notepad, crushing the paper with his fingers and thumb before throwing it into the bayou.

From out of the corner of his eye, Tom saw the city worker shaking his head. The man had seen what Tom had done.

"Trash can!" the worker shouted. Tom looked down the bank at the man's scowling face as the worker used his stick to point at a public trash can.

Tom turned back to the bayou and watched the paper drift for a moment in the current until the water took it under.

Tom tore out the final page and crumpled it up into a ball. He tossed it out farther into the bayou. After it hit the water, the ball of paper floated there for a few seconds, trying to open like a flower, like a small chrysanthemum.

"Just a minute!" the man shouted again. The man started coming toward Tom, using the stick, almost like a cane.

Tom turned in the other direction. He carried the blank notepad back to his car.

The Cake Box
By Cecilia Kennedy

A white box, sprinkled with frozen ice crystals, sits right in the middle of the freezer. It has been there since the day that Richard and I moved in. It came with a note loosely taped to the top. It said, "Wedding cake top and topper. Do not remove."

"Time to get rid of *this*," Richard said when he saw it.

"No—no, you can't. It's bad luck," I said.

"Yeah, but it's taking up space."

"Right. There's no room for all of the sides of beef we store and eat."

"Okay, okay. I know—we don't need to store massive sides of beef, but it can't be good—leaving food like that in the freezer. For how long? Kind of gross."

"Forget about it," I said, while closing the door. "Out of sight. Out of mind."

And, for a long time, we never talked about the old, old wedding cake in our freezer. Over the next few months, we shoved popsicles, ice cream, frozen veggies, and microwavable meals into the freezer—just placing items around the box—sometimes on top of it. We became quite used to seeing that box every day. We had never really opened it, either. We just assumed that the box contained a wedding cake top and topper.

After a few more months, Richard fell into a routine at work and I fell into my own routine at home—dividing my day between several part-time online gigs, small writing projects, and customer service jobs. This house seemed to have a generic, sterile feeling, but as I spent more time in this house, in long stretches of silence, I began to feel a kind of change take over. I couldn't quite explain it. The air around me started to feel slightly heavier, and I began to think I saw shadows out of the corners of my eye, but when I'd look, nothing would be there. Still, I felt like I was being watched in the doorways, the hallway, and the bedroom. Something waited on the stairs. Something watched from the windows.

One night, when Richard came home late, I convinced him to stay up with me and finish off a bottle of wine. When the crisp sweet Riesling made the edges of the room bend and sway, I suggested we open the cake box.

"We should get rid of the cake and the cake box while we're at it," Richard said.

"No, I just want to open it. What flavor do you think it is? Chocolate? Lemon? Strawberry? I'll bet it has buttercream frosting! I hope it's buttercream!"

"What? Shelly! Are you planning on tasting the cake?"

"Why not?"

"Oh, there are lots of reasons why not."

I got up from the kitchen table and grabbed a fork from the drawer and slammed it down on the counter-top as a challenge.

"Okay, okay. I see where this is going," Richard said.

He rose from the table too and returned with another bottle of wine, a knife, another fork, two plates, and a napkin.

"Game on," he said.

"All right—here are the rules: The one to eat the most cake without getting sick is exempt from making the bed for the next two weeks."

"Whatever," Richard replied, knowing full well that he'd end up making the bed anyway because our other rule for making the bed is the following: Whoever gets out of bed last is the one who has to make the bed and Richard always gets up last.

The glint in his eyes dared me to make the next move. So, I walked over to the freezer, pulled open the door, and brought the cake box back over to the table. The box felt cold, but heavy. The paper-thin cardboard on all three sides was stiff and brittle. It wasn't hard to flip the top of the box open. By now, any tape that might have been stuck to the bottom was useless in holding it together. But when I flipped the top open, Richard and I jumped back—our eyes wide open. There, staring straight up at us, were two dark purple shadows that covered the half-closed eyes of a frozen head. The eyebrows were thick with frost. The stringy, thin hair was still plastered to the pale face of a woman, darkened in purple shapes where blood must have once flowed.

"Oh my God! Call the police—call them now! Now!" Richard shouted.

I, on the other hand, refused to believe it was real. This couldn't have possibly been real at all.

"Just hold on. We don't know for sure if it's a human head. It could be one of those cakes—those super realistic cakes—like you see on baking shows. I'm going to try slicing into it."

"Oh my God, no!"

"Just relax. I'll bet it's all cake and we'll have a good laugh."

"I can't watch! I'm not watching."

While Richard covered his eyes, I picked up a chef's knife to try to slice horizontally through the forehead.

"Ugh! It's super frozen. There are probably layers of cake and sugar all stuck together like rock. Richard, hold it steady while I cut."

"No—no way! It looks real. It's not cake, Shelly. It's not cake!"

"And I say it is. So, come on now. Hold the sides while I slice."

I pressed the blade down hard while Richard placed his trembling hands on either side of the head. I only managed to make a small dent into the forehead, and I couldn't tell if there was cake or human tissue underneath.

"We're going to have to thaw it out a little," I said.

"No—no we're not. We're done, Shelly. Done! I mean, smell it. Do you smell it? Now that the top is open? Now that you've seen it?"

I did seem to smell something foul and pungent—something ripe and sickening. My own skin started to creep with the realization that I had attempted to slice into a frozen human severed head. I threw the knife into the sink and washed my hands under searing hot water— my mind racing.

"We can't call the police," I finally told Richard. "It's late. We're drunk and I just tried to slice into a frozen head, thinking it was a cake. A cake, Richard! What would the police think? We can't call them now. Let's just put it back in the freezer. We'll figure out what to do with it tomorrow. Maybe we'll just bury it or something."

"How? How will we be able to sleep, knowing there's a frozen head in our freezer?"

"We've slept pretty well so far. Tonight, will be no exception."

However, when I lifted the corners of the bed covers and slid under the sheets next to Richard, I still smelled that pungent, dead odor. It penetrated the sheets, my hair, and the skin of my hands. It hung like a cloud over the two of us. I tossed and turned thinking about the dead, cold eyes—the dark, gray, pale, and putrid skin. Did she suffer? Who put her there? Who was she? Richard tossed and turned too, but eventually he fell asleep. I could hear him softly snoring.

I closed my eyes tightly. Eventually, I began to dream. A place, that somehow felt familiar, but that I didn't quite recognize, came into view. I was there, walking. The place was near a river of sorts, next to a vibrant street of markets, restaurants, and music. Instinctively, I knew that if I turned to my right, there would be a wide, gravel-lined tunnel. And there it was—just as I had remembered. The sky was overcast in this place and I was a foreigner here—in Spain. I was in Spain again as a study-abroad student. The smells of olive oil and rich pastries floated in the air as I walked through the tunnel. I expected the tunnel to take me on a shortcut through the plaza, just as I'd done many times before during my stay, but instead of the plaza, I saw a busy highway, filled with buses and cars. The anxious feeling of being lost consumed me. Turning back was probably the best option I had, but when I turned around, the tunnel was no longer there. Instead, I was looking down, from above, unaware of how I'd gotten there. Below me, I could see dark red pools of blood drenching the light gray gravel pieces on the ground. The air felt unnaturally cold. And then I saw it: a body lying on the ground, lifeless—a child killed in a hit-and-run accident. I'd seen him before, but only in an instant, when I had rented a car to go exploring—and couldn't stop in time when a small figure ran into my car's path. I remembered a blur of striped shirt, a solid frame, the lace of a shoe, the horrid sound of a body crumpling, and the unmistakable jolt of the car. I just kept going. I told myself it was nothing—all of these years. Nothing. I'd never even told Richard. I'd never thought about what remained in my memory—never tried to give it a voice. But it had one. The child's body, oozing blood into the gravel, began to twitch and jerk mechanically, as if jolted by some unnatural source of electricity. It cracked its neck to turn and look at me. And the face—the face transformed from that of an eleven-year-old boy to a frost-bitten, icy face, which floated above me, its eyes half closed. In that moment, I recognized that face as well.

"Shelly," it said, in its otherworldly voice. "Leave me alone! Leave me alone, or your dreams will be the same every night. You'll wander this same path, over and over again. Leave well enough alone!"

When I awoke, my pajamas were soaked in sweat. I felt feverish, but cold at the same time. When I turned to look at Richard, he was staring up at the ceiling, his eyes wide with fear.

"What is it?" I asked. "Richard! What's happening?"

"There's something I've never told you. Something I've tried to hide all of these years, but I just dreamed it now."

"It's okay, Richard. You can tell me."

"I once had a little brother. He was so annoying. We were out swimming in a lake, and I was daring him to hold his breath under water. Shelly, I was incredibly jealous of him. Everyone seemed to like him best. He was funny, athletic—everything I wanted to be. I couldn't stand it. But he couldn't hold his breath as long as I could under water, so I said I'd help him. I'd help him build up the endurance to be able to hold his breath. And you know what I did? You know what I did to help him? I held his head under water, until he stopped moving. Then, I told everyone it was an accident—and they believed me. All of these years."

I held Richard close and told him that everything was going to be okay—that he didn't have to tell anyone. He was just a child. He didn't have to relive his past over and over again. I told him about my dream, where the frozen head visited me and gave a warning. I told him to just keep the head in the freezer and all would be well. As long as the head stayed in the freezer—and we told no one—we wouldn't have these dreams anymore.

And it worked. For nearly three weeks, we dreamed of forests, sunrises, and fields of flowers. But then . . . the head in the freezer wanted more. She demanded that we take her out of the freezer to talk to her. I decided to take that burden on my shoulders, since I worked from home. I would take her out for afternoon tea. A ritual—that's what she needed perhaps. A tea-time ritual to break up the day. During our tea-time rituals, she told me her name was Noreen and that she loved this house so now, she didn't want to leave it. I didn't mind entertaining Noreen, but she was so incredibly needy. I'd just sit her head on a plate in the middle of the kitchen table, pour the tea, and endure an hour of conversations that would go something like this:

"So, Shelly, what do you have planned today?"

"Oh, not much, Noreen—just some projects and contract work. And you?"

"I hear these voices all of the time. They tell me I should leave, but I'm not going anywhere. Can you turn me to the left a little? The sunlight through the window is starting to melt my face a bit."

"Sure. I'll turn you just a little here. And those voices, you don't want to listen to them?"

"Oh, heavens no! I know who they are."

"And who are they, then?"

"People who've moved on. People who hate me—who want to see me suffer. They claim I've taken their lives too soon—my own children, even. But we were only playing. Just games. That's all it was."

"What kind of games?"

"Hide and seek—with knives. It was great fun that taught survival skills. One of the little buggers found me though. That's how I ended up here—in a cake box. But that's okay. I'll just stay put."

"Yes, indeed you will . . . Well, time's up. Back in the freezer you go!"

But one day, Noreen stopped me.

"No. Before you put me back in, I'd like for you to promise me that you'll start taking me out twice a day. Once for tea and once for dinner with you and Richard. I'd like to talk to Richard too. I hardly ever see him."

Eventually, I started to take Noreen out of the freezer at dinner time. She even helped to plan the weeknight menu. She liked to watch us eat. Richard could barely tolerate her.

"My God, Noreen! If I have to hear about the hide-and-seek with knives story one more time, I'm going to scream. And can we at least cover your face while we eat? It's getting worse. The freezing and thawing going on between your daily visits is wearing down the skin in a most unappetizing manner."

Noreen was very hurt by Richard's words. I had to remind him to have more respect because she had the power to turn our dreams into painful memories.

It has been two years since we've been taking Noreen out of the freezer twice a day for conversations and I'm two months pregnant with my first child. I haven't told Noreen yet, but I think she suspects something, and I feel a kind of sadness wash over me—knowing that this child will never be able to invite friends over for dinner.

The Guacamole and Frosé Party
By Cecilia Kennedy

At the front steps of suburbia's interpretation of the massive, modern Swiss chalet, I hear muffled laughter and the shuffle of fashionable shoes on shiny wooden floors. I ring the doorbell. The sip 'n paint party Rochelle has arranged must be in full swing. Maybe I got the time wrong. I ring the doorbell again. No one answers, so I try the door—and walk right in. Very awkward. Shouting, "The party's here now," is so wrong, but I do it anyway. No one hears me. The air is heavy with perfume and I want to choke. The label on the lit candle in the middle of the foyer says, "Ocean Breeze," but it's more like a slap in the face with laundry soap.

To the right, is where I hear voices and high-pitched laughter. I also hear the sound of some kind of machine, perhaps a blender, going at full strength. To the right then, must be the kitchen. Though I swing the door wide open with a bang, no one notices. The guests are too busy eating guacamole, chips, and some kind of pink slushy concoction—a "frosé" I think.

"Ainsley!" Rochelle says, when she finally sees me reaching for a handful of chips to swipe into the largest bowl of green, lumpy avocado mush I've ever seen.

"You *must* have a frosé. It's *the* drink of the summer," she says.

I put the drink to my lips and admit to myself that it's not bad at all—for a girly drink. It's not the crappy beer I usually guzzle, but I like it. I can taste the wine and a hint of strawberries—and now, I really hate to admit it, but I think the drink could be sweeter. And, should it be served with guacamole? No one cares. Instead, everyone's ooing and ahhing over the cute aprons Rochelle has taken the time to make for each one of her guests. The aprons are covered in hand-painted flowers, and it's clear to me: We're not just here to drink and laugh. We're here to create art, and I'm not an artist. I down three more frosés and fight the brain freeze. Rochelle passes out perfectly clean ceramic bowls, plates, and other dishes. We can help ourselves to brushes, specially designed ceramic paints, and glasses of water for cleaning off the brushes.

"So, Rochelle—will we get some kind of a lesson first?"

"Oh, no! No lessons! This is just *fun.*"

But I only see women here with their game faces on. Whatever they're planning, I definitely can't compete. Instead, I grab a bowl and paint the whole thing in blue. It takes me all of five minutes.

"There. Done," I tell Rochelle.

My fingers are covered in paint, which I've somehow managed to smear all over the cute little apron.

"No, Ainsley. You can't just paint something one color. This is a chance to explore—to see what you've got inside you."

To my surprise, some of the women at the party, who didn't look like they could doodle squat, have already painted meticulous designs—including entire landscapes on the body of ceramic dragons and cups.

"Maybe I'll test out a design on paper first," I say.

So, I find a stray cocktail napkin and begin to dip my finger into the paint and make thumbprints. With a black pen, I then attempt to make fins, eyes, and tails in order to transform my thumbprints into fish, but I soon discover that I can't even do that. The fins, I suppose, are based on a triangle shape, but I have problems positioning the triangle onto the body at a proper angle. The eyes are too big, and the mouths look like Pepperidge Farm Goldfish smiles, which are more "cutesy" than artistic. I end up just drawing scribbles and random lines here and there and, by the time I'm done, the fish look more like ridiculous blobs with spikes. The dull, sleepy effects of the alcohol have also taken over by now and I no longer care about making art. Before I know it, my head has dropped to the table and I'm falling asleep-drooling on my fish blobs—breathing in and out deeply through my mouth and nose. I hope I'm not snoring, but I probably am.

A vague buzz of laughter bounces all around me in long, far-off echoes. I'm aware that I'm not dreaming of anything in particular. In fact, I can still feel things, like an annoying, slimy itchy sensation that tickles both of my nostrils. Perhaps now, mucous is falling from my nose onto the cocktail napkin as I sleep-snore, but I'm too tired to lift my head from the table. The guests carry on without me.

The tickling, slimy feeling in my nostrils continues, and now, it's sliding down the back of my throat. I can no longer stay asleep; I'm becoming more and more aware of some kind of movement in my throat. Something is moving around in my esophagus and it seems to be solid, bumping back and forth against the inner structure of my throat. Its movement chokes me, and I begin to emerge from sleep, clutching at my neck. Standing up, I look around. The other guests are busy making their artwork—discussing how maybe they'll sell their crafts on Etsy or something, or open up a side business.

"Oh, Rochelle!" they say. "Thank you for being such an empowering friend!"

Meanwhile, I'm pounding my fist into my chest as hard as I can. The other alternative, I believe, is to throw myself down onto the back of a chair and hope that the impact dislodges whatever it is that's trapped inside me. Yet, I think I can still breathe, so maybe I can just keep pounding on my chest. Eventually, the other guests turn to look at me, and I realize I'm the most misbehaved one here. I've fallen asleep on a cocktail napkin and I've woken up choking.

"Are you okay?" Rochelle asks.

The slimy mass slides down my throat and lodges in my chest, where it continues to move and wriggle about. It's extremely uncomfortable—like heartburn mixed with acid reflux, burning my chest and throat, but at least I can breathe and talk.

"Let's see what you've been working on," she says.

I look around at the vases, cups, and plates the other women have painted. They're overflowing with brilliant color, which drenches the landscapes, gardens, and portraits these women have lovingly created. Anything and everything I've done up until now is supremely inferior.

"Come on—just pick up your napkin and show us. It's totally fine. You're among friends here," Rochelle says.

But when I look down at the cocktail napkin, nothing is there. The blobby fish with misshapen eyes, tails, and fins, are gone.

"There's nothing there," I say. "I've got nothing."

The other women in the room look at one another and give me a sympathetic pout.

"You *do* have something," Rochelle says, while putting her arm around my shoulder to comfort me. "Deep inside you," she says, tapping her finger over my heart.

In response, that something inside me jumps and wriggles with great force. I have to try to steady myself at the table.

"We all have something inside of us—something to give," Rochelle says. "It's just untapped potential we need to find."

Rochelle looks around at all of the other guests, and they nod their heads at one another—like they hold some kind of secret, which they will soon share with me.

"Let's show her. Shall we?" Rochelle says.

I'm not really sure what's going to happen, but it seems like they're all ganging up on me—like they all belong to some kind of secret sisterhood they've built without me. And I'm supposed to just stand there and watch—and hope that somehow, I belong too.

Rochelle pulls a chair into the middle of the room.

"I'll go first," she says.

I watch as she squats down over the chair and reaches up under dress to pull her underpants down. I can't believe what I'm seeing. I don't know whether to run away or to laugh hysterically, but I just stand there with my mouth open. I watch as Rochelle's face turns bright red and disfigured as she strains and pushes in order to expel something onto the chair. I'm beginning to think that I know what that something might be, and I don't really want to see it. I don't want to watch each guest take turns dumping onto a chair. Just when I'm about to turn on my heels and run, Rochelle's face returns to normal and she discreetly pulls her underpants back on. Stepping away from the chair, she reveals what came out of her: Fine silver threads, delicate and beautiful.

"This runs in my family," she says. "I come from a family of weavers of fine cloth. It's pure silver—very valuable."

I just nod my head in amazement. Truly, I'm stunned.

The next guest hovers over the chair to groan and grunt. From her, sapphires appear. "They bring wisdom," she says.

All of the guests take turns on the chair—expelling nothing but valuable treasures. Then, they all turn around at once and look at me.

"It's your turn," they say.

I don't like the way they're looking at me, but I don't think I can leave, either. My throat is still burning, but now my pulse is racing. If I could run past them and get to the door, I would, but I get the feeling that they won't let me. In fact, they're closing in around me—making me the center of their circle. I'm breathing harder and faster now. A cold, clammy hand falls firmly on my right shoulder. One of the guests has me in her grip.

"We all have something to give," she says, icily in my ear.

"I don't think I have anything good to give," I say.

"Everyone does," Rochelle replies—and they all repeat it as a chant: Everyone does. Everyone does. Everyone does.

The slimy mass inside me squirms and burns my esophagus. I can feel the acid rising—the bile building—forcing my mouth open. I convulse and heave, like I'm about to vomit.

"It's coming!" Rochelle says. "It's coming!"

They all gather around to peek inside my mouth, while I clutch again at my throat—and retch.

"I think I see it," someone says.

A chunky mixture of pink and green splats onto the wooden floor. The women jump back, but bits and pieces fall onto their summer dresses. They dab at themselves daintily with cocktail napkins and gingerly step around the vomited pile in the middle of the floor.

"It's just guacamole and frosé," I say.

"Nope. I see something else," Rochelle says.

She returns to the kitchen and gets a pair of rubber gloves. Then, she stoops down to pick through the chunks of guacamole and watery bits of tortilla chips. From the mess, she pulls an odd-shaped piece that appears to be wriggling—and I recognize it immediately—especially when Rochelle struggles to keep it still while she wipes it clean. It's one of the blobby fish I made earlier.

"Did you make this?" Rochelle asks.

"Yes—on the cocktail napkin, but it's not there anymore."

Rochelle puts a hand to her mouth, like she's trying to stifle a laugh, but she can't.

"It must have crawled inside you while you were passed out drunk!"

The rest of the women break into laughter.

"*That's* what's inside you!" they say, while still laughing and holding their sides.

I don't really care for it. I'm incredibly insulted.

"I'll just grab my things and I'll leave," I say.

I stoop over the guacamole mass and extract, one by one, the slippery blobs of misshapen fish—all done up in yellow, blue, brown, orange, red, pink, and purple. I place them into a jar and take them home. At home, I find a necklace chain and string them onto it.

In my closet, I find a white sundress—the perfect canvass for my necklace. I go over to the light of the setting sun and watch as the fragments shine through the fish—as if they were pieces of jade and sea glass on sand. Stepping out onto the sidewalk in front of my house, I turn right. A little girl on her bicycle pedals past—and I wave. She slows down.

"Can I see your necklace?" she asks.

I bend down towards her so that she can take the chain into her hands and examine it. She runs her fingers over the smooth shapes.

"Cool," she says.

"Thanks. I made it myself. Didn't know I had it in me."

Half Witch
By Charlie Lefever

Last weekend I went to my friend's birthday party. Or, at least, I tried to. I had just come from work and I was anxious to get to the party. I wanted to see my friends. They had moved recently and when I got to the address I was given, the place looked dark. I checked my phone, checked the street signs. This was definitely it. I walked up the couple concrete steps, opened the screen door, and tried the handle. It was locked. I turned and went quickly back to the sidewalk. Then I see the curtain move and notice a woman peering at me. She had a wild, angry look in her eye and she was muttering to herself. I gave a half wave, thinking she might let me in. But she disappeared behind the curtain. The woman re-appeared a couple seconds later, leaning with her head and shoulders out of the screen door. Her eyes were hard and set, her blonde hair big and messy around her small face.

"What are you doing here?" She threw her words at me.

"I'm sorry, I'm just lookin for my friend's house and this is the address I was given."

"You came into my vestibule."

"I know, I didn't mean to scare you, I just thought my friend lived here."

"Okay," she said, hard and unforgiving, as if she didn't believe me in the slightest. I could tell I'd woken her up. She was angry, her energy a pulsing red she threw at me. But I knew what was underneath. Yellow. She was afraid.

"Really," I said, my hands out in front of me. "Really, I mean you no harm."

"Okay," she said again, still hard, though her eyes softened just the slightest. And then she was gone. I walked away, feeling horrible that I'd frightened her.

Because I know what it's like. I'm half witch. I've been scared and had my powers flare up inside of me, eyes wild, hair a mess, ready to spit incantations at the man threatening to harm me. But that night, I was one of them. A man pacing on the sidewalk in front of a woman's house. Walking up her front steps, lurking in her vestibule. I could tell by the way she looked at me, body tense, ready to defend herself, that she didn't recognize me as a member of the coven. It's been happening more and more, as I float in the in-between space of man and woman, mortal and witch. Every so often I'm on the receiving end of that witch force, a force created by generations of drownings and burnings, our powers pushed down deep inside of us for fear of persecution. And every time I feel that force, it makes me ache. I ache for every woman that has had a strange man pace in front of her house at night. For every woman that has bowed her head and kept her eyes low for fear of what her eye contact might trigger in a man. For every woman that has dared to show her powers only to be crushed into silence by the weight of a mortal. I want to gather them all up, run a hand through their wild hair and reassure them, *really, I mean you no harm.*

White Sunlight Coming In
By Charlie Lefever

The day I lost my virginity, I cried. Adam and I talked about when it would be. I was a virgin. He wasn't. I had been properly conditioned. I wanted it to be, at least a little bit, special.

Our first try was five months into dating. We went to an Italian restaurant for dinner. I had never been in love before. I thought this was love. It wasn't.

I tried to crystalize the moment by decorating. I plugged in twinkle lights. We hung up bed sheets to create a hiding place. I played Iron and Wine in the background.

It didn't work. I was too dry. He didn't take the time to make me wet. We tried in vain for a few minutes. Then he rolled off me. He said it was okay, that we'd try again another time. We fell asleep in our fort.

—

A few weeks later is when it happened. Adam decided to take matters into his own hands. My one shot at something special had passed. There were no twinkle lights this time, no fort, no crooning of Iron and Wine. We were on my bed, white sunlight coming in from the window behind it. He stood over me, his feet on the floor. I laid sprawled on the bed. And he thrusted. Over. And. Over. Like pounding a fist into a baseball glove to break it in. Deep, rhythmic thrusts. I looked up at him. He stared down between my legs and watched himself take my virginity. I laid still until it was over.

After, he laid down next to me. I rolled away and began to cry. I had no words for the emotions fighting for space in my chest. Years later, tender sex cracked open the hard shell that had formed around those emotions and the words finally came pouring out.

Shame.

Guilt.

Worthlessness.

I had known Adam for awhile now. We were in a committed relationship. I thought I wasn't supposed to feel this way. So I decided I didn't feel this way.

And yet, I cried. I had hated it. I hadn't felt a single thing. No spark, no deep connection, no overwhelming joy. Only pain. And loneliness.

Adam came to comfort me. He asked me what was wrong. I shook my head. He told me no more crying after sex. I nodded. He told me he was hungry, so we got dressed. I put my flower patterned sundress over my shame and my guilt and I pretended like nothing had happened.

The Season's Wife
By Emily Strauss

in the mirror between breaths she appears
stripped naked in winter, standing under
the moon, her ghostly skin shining

between breaths she appears, puffs of steam
from her lips, she stands in the snow alone
she waits silently, smelling the wind, waits

for the old man bent and wrinkled, white
hair blowing, she watches him fly down
a huge owl soft-winged on the branch

a mirror to the night shining in her shallow
eyes, one silence holds them both—
invisible wife, owl fixed in the snow.

On Demand of Death

--on the death of RP in a motorcycle accident
By Emily Strauss

I can't force a poem into the light
any more than a body, once the soul is gone.

All that remains are massive internal injuries
under a white sheet on the side of a road.

Let me set words down on paper
a metaphor for crushed bones.

Nor can I compel a poem to form
like doctors can't close a seam

in flesh mangled beyond recognition.
I could impose rhymes on hapless words

ignore spilled blood in the weeds.
I don't know how to write

a poem of death when suddenly someone's
gone and the road is empty.

Maybe I could find a phrase by the curve
where the glass has been swept up

but not the echo of a laugh.
These ashes so light in their polished chest.

I'll Have a Number 3 Please, Hold the Memories
By Emma Demski

Driving in our rental car down the Texas highway, everything appeared to be the same. Except. Not. There were little differences. The highways were new, and somehow were made more terrifying. They were 50 feet up in the air and looped around like a horrifying free-for-all rollercoaster. My dad would throw in a loving 'yee-haw' whenever he made an especially tight turn. The Super Target got a new sign, and the McDonald's right by the furniture store, Freed's, went out of business. But, the sun-faded orange roof of Whattaburger was still there. As well as the unfortunately named, Fuzzy Taco, that we never went to. We left the snow-covered trees of Michigan for a welcoming 70 degrees. I wore capri-pants while the locals donned wool sweaters. It was the first time I had been back since my family had become fractured. Addison was specifically where we always stayed and was where my brother Colin used to live. My mom and I tagged along to attend the holiday party for my dad's company, like we used to.

A town within Dallas county, Addison was known for its sheer number of restaurants per square mile. I went for the first time in 4th grade when my dad's wire manufacturing business opened up the new location, and Colin moved down from Michigan to help start the branch. Most of the restaurants looked unassuming from the exterior, with old paint jobs and worn front doors, but the food was homey and hypnotizing. Addison wasn't pretty or scenic. There weren't any majestic waterfalls or elaborate monuments, it wasn't a postcard worthy vacation spot. Addison was filled with strip malls and sad heat-stricken trees holding on for dear life; it was a commercialized and chain-restaurant heaven, and I loved it.

Growing up, I enjoyed going to Addison for the food— we didn't have the same chains in Michigan— but mostly to see Colin. He would always show us a weird new area, or we would end up at some random cowboy festival. We would drive all over Texas, down to San Antonio to check out the Alamo or to Austin to hear live music. The landscapes of our drives were flat and overwhelmingly beige; the trips were long and monotonous, with the always blindingly blue sky, which made naps a challenge. There were the infrequent patches of wild sunflowers on the side of the road, that my mom always pointed out with one hand over her heart. Colin and I were in the backseat, leaning against each other, our freckled arms chilled by the air conditioning, reading our own respective books. Mine probably had some animal as the protagonist, and his was most likely a biography about some niche 80s techno band. These longer trips were usually just for the weekend, since Colin had to return to work on Monday morning.

We frequently went to Fort Worth, which was much closer to Addison, they had an old-timey cowboy town there. You could take a picture with a real longhorn, the one of me was displayed in our living room back in Michigan. We weren't limited to Addison, it was our home base, our familiar place for dinner. During the day, we could go just about anywhere. One time, Colin found a park two hours away that had preserved dinosaur footprints. He loved how eccentric Texas was, and so did I. Colin was also a ginger, so the two of us had this inherent connection, even if he was 18 years older than me. He also hated eggs and mustard and pickles.

After my parents and I checked into our hotel, we made our way to The Blue Goose, which was right down the street, the epicenter of Addison itself. It was one of the reasons that we stayed in that specific area of Dallas originally. Rachel Ray went there on one of her old Food Network shows and gave her approval to the sour cream enchiladas. The Demskis agreed. The restaurant was decorated in bright 90s colors: teals, blues, pinks, oranges, greens, just like the title card of *The Fresh Prince of Bel-Air*, which I always used to watch in our hotel room. This restaurant was our first stop on each vacation.

On a typical trip, it would have been the five of us: myself, my parents, Colin and his wife (and eventually my niece once she was born). I would sneakily read a book under the table or play my Nintendo DS, while they would discuss taxes or savings bonds: whatever *adults* talked about. I would usually nag my brother to help me get through a difficult Mario Brothers level, tugging on his brown striped shirt. He didn't know the controls very well, so he was never much help.

This time it was just my parents and me. I was now 20, and I hadn't been here since I was a freshman in high school. The restaurant was dead since it was 2 o'clock in the afternoon on a Wednesday. The three of us flipped through our menus even though we all knew our orders. I sat across from my parents, who were inverses of each other. My mom 5 foot 4 in her black-patent Birkenstocks and my dad over 6 feet in his bright white Adidas. We ordered queso and we dipped into the sizzling cheese with fresh chips. My mom as if on cue spilled some on her shirt. It wasn't a Demski meal until my mom ended up with a food stain on her clothes. As we ate, I couldn't help but feel an uneasiness in my stomach. I kept expecting to see Colin shuffle in through the front door and sit down with us. I could barely glance at the sizzling neon-beer signs without hearing his wheezy laugh that jiggled his shoulders. He left an oily remain all over the town.

I'd been removed from this place for so long and now I was painfully trying to fit myself back in like a semi-closed up piercing. We went over our plans for the next four days among the wafts of sharp chili-peppers; we were planning on doing all of the things we normally did. There wasn't really anything new to do in Addison.

"I'm pretty sure that we've sat in this booth before," my mom said as she whirled her straw around in her iced tea.

"I would imagine that we've sat just about everywhere in this restaurant," my dad said, taking off his University of Michigan hat, running his fingers through his short gray hair. "Yeah, we have. I remember." I tapped the plastic orange tablecloth.

Colin moved back to Michigan, out of nowhere, when I was in the 7th grade. I didn't know anyone else with siblings that old growing up, so I thought that all adult siblings were unsettled, still trying to find themselves. He came to live with us at the end of my freshman year of high school after falling on hard times. My parents were open to help him out and I loved having him at home because I felt like I truly had a brother since I saw him every day. He would take me to flea markets and play me the odd techno music he made in our basement. He burned me CDs of music he thought I would like and begrudgingly also all of John Mayer's discography. I always knew he was strange, that's why him and I got along so well. I shelved most of my peculiar interests at school, but at home, he always got the full me.

Then one day in February, during my sophomore year of high school, he was gone. Now six years later, I still haven't had any contact with him. Every time I saw a ginger-haired man on the street, I double checked to see if it was him. I was still in the habit of doing this. At the time, I didn't even know the questions to ask, so I didn't. I thought that it was somehow my fault, and I felt ashamed, especially since we were so close. He was sleeping in the bedroom right next to mine, but there was a lot I didn't know. For the first three years he was gone, I didn't even know if he was still alive. I looked online for *some* answers but found nothing. There have been a few brief phone calls and one meeting between him and one of our other brothers. All I knew now was that he somehow made his way to Florida, and I was not going to be seeing him anytime soon. He had always been eccentric and had a sporadic nature about him. His initial move to Addison was fairly last minute. He only decided a few months before he drove down with our dad in the large white company van with a hamster in the back, but that's another story. I knew that there were tensions about money, and a rising conflict with him and his (now ex) wife, but these little, poorly knitted threads were all that I had.

***

There was now an In-N-Out burger right off the main street in Addison. None of us had ever been to one before, since they were usually on the West Coast. After my dad got off of work, we drove over and were greeted by the stark white and red décor. "They have strawberry shakes, so I'm happy," my dad said, looking up at the menu. We were all pretty easy to please— Demskis weren't notoriously picky eaters. Once we sat down, myself across from my parents, we all immediately began eating.

"The fries are pretty good!" my mom said, fluffing her dyed blonde hair.

"The sweet tea is quite solid," I said.

"Sweet enough to chew?" my dad asked. He too liked a hearty glass of Texas sweet tea, the kind that had soup-ladles full of sugar. I nodded. "Do you remember that place in San Antonio?" My dad sucked on his shake. "Rudy's? They proclaimed to be the 'Worst Barbeque in Texas."

"Yeah, that place sold creamed corn by the pint, it was awesome," I said. We only went because we were bombarded by billboards on the highway. It was in the middle of nowhere and you had to sit on rickety picnic tables outside, but the food was absolutely delicious.

"You got your meat on butcher paper, they practically threw it to you. They didn't care! It was so..." he paused.

"Texas. You could only have that place here," my mom filled in.

"It's kind of crazy that I remember everything, like, all of the streets and places," I said. The burgers and fries weren't bad, they just didn't fit into the landscape. The restaurant looked too new and fresh. It wasn't worn by people and memories yet. Colin had never been here.

"We used to come here a lot, it makes sense. Addison hasn't really changed all that much," my mom said. She adjusted her glasses as she took my discarded pickles that I plucked off my burger. No one talked about Colin, at least not around me. In the years following his leave, his name was probably brought up no more than ten times. I had to assume a lot and do my own detective work. Even here, his name was poisonous. I technically had four older brothers, but I kept wondering if I should just change it to three.

On one of the many previous Texas trips, I spent the night at Colin's apartment with him and his wife, while my parents went to a business dinner. The two of them took me to get Mexican food and we gorged ourselves on beef tacos: the good ones, that came with two small corn tortillas. We listened to "Weird" Al in the car, another one of our shared interests. Colin and I sang along to every word of "Amish Paradise" as he drove, his wife was unamused. That night we went to an arcade located in a strip mall in between a tattoo studio and a soon-to-be closing Chinese restaurant. They had a whole room full of old-school arcade games that all took nickels. He knew most of the games by their artwork, all of them were brand new to my eyes. I thought this was an exciting night on the town, not just a cheap activity for my brother to do with me. That night we went swimming in his apartment complex's pool. We ate frozen Twix bars to stay cool, almost chipping our teeth on the icy caramel. On summer nights, Texas was still in the 90s.

It was so easy to want to paint Colin as a villain in my mind— just throw some devil horns on him and toss him aside. He wasn't always the most stand-up guy. When he left us, he also left behind his own daughter and ex-wife. He now has a new girlfriend (possibly wife) and a new son. It's unlikely that he's been paying child support. Looking back, he would commonly leave his jobs and sporadically move away. He briefly lived in Pennsylvania and Indiana, with my niece and his ex-wife. They would never stay long, and he would always find himself pulling into our circle driveway. I thought this was going to happen again this time, too. My parents haven't moved, but this possibility seems to propel itself further away with each day.

The memories of us watching dumb made-for-tv movies or going to resale shops to find the most outlandish thing always swirled back. I could picture him easily: his crazy curly hair that gathered into tufts on his head, signaling the necessity for a haircut and his bright blue eyes underneath his wire-frame glasses. It was his voice, though; that's where my memory faltered. I remembered his clothes: lots of brown pants and graphic tees adorned with irreverent jokes. I couldn't really remember the way he used to say certain words, though. I wasn't sure if my memory was trying to help or hurt me.

The holiday party took place in the ballroom of a hotel right off the freeway. The three of us dressed up. My dad in a dark charcoal suit, my mom in a nice blouse and black pants with the blue pearls my dad had gotten her for their thirtieth wedding anniversary, and I was wearing a dress I got from Target the week prior. My mom and I simultaneously gasped when we saw the lobby— everywhere we turned was purple velour and cheetah print. There were also large plastic jewels on everything: chandeliers, picture frames, chairs, lamps. The theme of the lobby bled into the party room. The tablecloths were a dark royal purple, coincidentally my dad's favorite color. My dad was probably compiling a list of jokes to rifle off later. Since my dad was the owner, he had to keep a professional composure. I was disgruntled that we were wasting one of our meals at a hotel buffet, but my dad suggested that we would grab dessert afterwards.

Even though most of the employees at the party were hired after Colin came back to Michigan, he was all I could think about. He would have loved to make fun of this place. I wanted to erase my brain of everything involving him. Could I coat-check my memories? They were getting in the way of my normal brain functions, squeezing my head like some sort of medieval torture device. Seeing his face now would be the equivalent of someone with a Scream mask popping out from behind a corner. This hotel was built after Colin left Addison. He was never even here. More and more of the ropes that kept me grounded in this town were being snipped away. I was left floating in this place where everywhere I looked, I felt pangs of deja-vu. Colin's freckle-sleeved arms couldn't bring me back down.

Before our flight that Saturday, we had to make a final stop at Braum's. They were a chain of fast food/dairies/small grocers around Texas and Oklahoma. My mom chose her traditional butter pecan and chocolate almond pairing; my dad got his festive pistachio and peppermint, and I had cookies and cream and double chocolate. As we ate our waffle cones, Christmas music leaked from the ceiling. I still had the last Christmas present he ever gave me: a red *Harry Potter* hoodie. He never read the books, but he knew how much they meant to me. We'd sat in the same exact plastic booth so many times before, the one right in the middle next to the frosted-glass divider.

"I think it's colder in here than it is outside!" I shivered from the air-conditioning. The vinyl cushion-backing was frigid on my bare arms.

"They don't want you to get overheated when you eat your ice-cream!" my dad said. My mom rolled her eyes.

I didn't tell my friends what had happened with Colin for years. I was embarrassed. Many of my friends knew him well, since he was always around the house. When they would ask where he was, I would usually just shrug and say that he was back in Indiana. He was like my twin that was almost two decades older than me. As I grew up without him, I mirrored him. I dyed my hair bright colors, collected vinyl and disappointed our parents by getting multiple tattoos. More recently, I've become resentful. I've gotten so much cooler since he left. I got my first pair of Dr. Martens the spring after he went M.I.A., discovered indie-rock music that summer, and became more interested in writing and existentialism the following year. I didn't even mean to copy him so closely; it just happened. I was angry that I was turning out like him, because I didn't want to follow his same path. Nonetheless, I still felt the urge to talk to him, wishing I had some sort of contact available when I found a cool new music video. These impulses were simply imagined conversations in my head. I wanted him to know me now.

As we drove our rental car to the Dallas-Fort-Worth Airport, I realized how furious I was at him. He ruined this trip, my ghost of a brother that I mourned, although we never held a funeral. He was unflinchingly living his second life in Florida. I wasn't sure how to react if I were to see him again. Part of me would want to slap him and rip out his hair. Another would prefer to say silent, walking away. A third would yearn to pick up exactly where we left off. I hated myself for fantasizing about such encounters, because I had already pushed him so far out of my life. As we passed by all of the familiar stores and establishments that were staples of my childhood, I felt like a fraud in this town. I had forgotten whether his name had one 'l' or two.

Assistant ² City Manager
By Emma Demski

Jane walked carefully down the block heading towards her parent's house in the outskirts of Old Yolk City, defeated after a less than successful time campaigning at a local butcher shop. Her limp green backpack contained a neat stack of hand-folded pamphlets, two-inch by two-inch circle stickers, some granola bar wrappers and a cow pencil case. Everything was printed in a bright white font with a pale lilac background: "Vote Whoopersmith for Assistant ² City Manager. Jane Covers Rock". It had the Rock, Paper, Scissors Party logo in the lower right-hand corner, a triangle with a rock at the top, a piece of paper on the lower left-hand side, and a pair of scissors on the right. The large city consisted of dozens of skyscrapers all jutting into the sky like butter knives. The prestigious Winebart Architecture Academy was to her left, which was named after Milton Winebart. Each graduating class collaborated and designed a new skyscraper to be added to the city— they were about five years away from running out of room. Because of all of the tall buildings, little sunlight was able to edge its way in, so the light posts were always on, except for an hour at midday. Toonsy Park, roughly ten blocks away, was dead center in the middle of the city and the only consistent place to get sun. Jane turned the corner on Ball-Creek Avenue right by the large LED billboard for Phillip's Yogurt Sticks, the one with an ominous giraffe mascot looking down on the citizens. She also passed a dangling flyer advertising the Duck-Run-About-Jamboree that was happening in a month and arrived at her parent's house with their sky-blue door.

She wore a purple dress with yellow tights. This was her power outfit, or at least she was trying to convince herself it was. She was only running for the Assistant *squared* position for Old Yolk City. After going to a rally sponsored by the RPS Party, she felt inspired as a recent college grad. The speakers' voices were bold and direct. They had the level of enthusiasm that her professors did. There was a curatorial job up at Center of the Communicative Arts, but she didn't get it. With her dreams devoured, she moved into a small apartment, with two lackluster roommates. She now worked a small paper shop, You Carbon Be Kidding Me. It wasn't perfect, but she loved the physicality of paper. She liked the crisp feel of cardstock between her fingertips. Her degree was in 20th Century British Printmaking, but she felt drawn to the small political position when she found out about the implications of the Dinali Pasta Tax. If it passed, her dad might lose his job as a supervisor for bowtie and cavatappi noodles that he had had for over fifteen years.

As soon as Jane walked in the door, she was greeted by the overwhelming cloud that was her mother, who was one of the best tour guides Forrest-Green Tour Company has ever seen. Her awards were carefully arranged on the small mantle in their living room.

"That was nice of Tony to let you do your little campaign thing," Jane's mother said as she set down a ceramic dish of green beans on the kitchen table. Jane went to have dinner with them at least once a week.

"He had no customers. He wasn't even fully stocked," Jane said, grabbing a dinner roll and passing the basket to her brother, Kevin.

Their father unbuttoned his work shirt, draping it on the back of his chair. He sat down in his undershirt, still with the faint rim of goggle lines around his eyes. Her mom brought over the turkey casserole and sat across from her husband. Kevin shoveled some of the steaming casserole onto his plate.

"I'm not going to win. I don't even know why I'm trying," Jane said, setting down her fork, only half of her turkey casserole eaten. Her stomach bubbled remembering the looks of the people at Tony's as they passed her over.

"Oh, honey, no, of course you're going to win!" said her mom. Kevin sighed. Her dad was quiet like usual, eating his food. He tried to be supportive, but he was a realist at heart.

"I don't have a cool or memorable name. That's what gets people elected," Jane said.

"That's not true!" her mom said. "We're the only Whoopersmiths in the city! We are, dare I say it, unique!" Her mom waved around a forkful of casserole with great enthusiasm.

"My name is Jane. There are thousands of Janes."

"Our Mayor's name is Toddlin Ruppers," said Kevin.

"Deppy *Silverjaw* is running against me. He's in the Beldan Sour Cream ™ party, so he has practically unlimited funding. RPS hasn't even officially sponsored me yet. That's why I'm doing this dumb campaigning thing, no one else has to do it because parents normally name their kids accordingly if they think they're going to be a politician!"

She was the only one running against Deppy. She had seen his name for years, since his dad was a pillar of the city council. One of his older brothers worked for Beldan Sour Cream ™. They didn't go to the same high school, but she had heard stories about him. Old Yolk City was fairly big, but everyone happened to know what you had for dinner last night and whether or not you had leftovers. She heard a rumor that he was a compulsive car theft at the age of twelve. Other people said that he is addicted to strawberry mints and ruined his father's credit because of it.

"We didn't know what you were going to be when you were born. Why should your name have any deciding factor? You're already separating yourself from the others, Jane," her dad said. "Go out and talk to people. If people aren't going to come to you, go to them." Jane turned to her food. Why should she have to do more work than the others? She'd give it one day. She had already been at it for a couple of weeks, unsure of how to assert herself into this unfamiliar world. She had stacks of unused stickers on her desk that reminded her of all of the people that didn't know her name yet.

The next morning Jane slipped on her slightly worn all-black orthopedic sneakers from her brief stint as a waitress in college. She collected her pamphlets and stickers, luckily, she got a significant employee discount and they had a really nice color printer at the shop. She wore dark pants and her medium-weight blue corduroy jacket to fight the early fall chill. As she walked out the door, she wasn't entirely sure *what* she was going to say. She practiced her points and her tone of voice in the shower that morning. She thought she sounded prepared, but then again, the acoustics in showers tend to make everything sound better.

"Hi, my name is Jane Whoopersmith and I'm running for Assistant [2] City Manager. Can I talk to you for a few minutes about my platform?" "Hi, my name is Jane and I'm with the Rock, Paper, Scissors Party, may I have some of your time?" "Are you planning to vote in the upcoming local election?"

"I'm not interested in politics." "I already know who I'm voting for." "I just go by the names." "Jane Whoopersmith? That's not a politicians' name."

Most people abruptly shut down the conversation or just slowly closed the door before she could finish. Jane started a few blocks from her house. The homes were tightly packed together, not as tall as the skyscrapers downtown, just simple brownstones with toast-colored bricks and neatly painted windows. It wasn't until the eighth house, that Jane had a legitimate interaction.

She had stayed up late the night before making sure that she was up to date with all of the main ballot initiatives including: mandatory healthcare for working animals, the widespread recognition of weasels as pets, and the large-scale movement of twins choosing to formally be recognized as one person. Her stances lined up almost exactly with the Rock, Paper, Scissors platform. The only plank that she differed from was from their stance on the twin one. Jane thought that personal individuality was important and that if more people started doing this there would be major tax and logistic complications.

"Sure, my morning radio program just ended," an older gentleman in a baggy flannel shirt said. He had a stack of wispy hair that waned like sea anemone. She was taken aback by the human interaction. She sputtered out a few indecipherable noises and handed him a pamphlet to buy her a few seconds to get her thoughts together.

"Awesome! Thank you—"

"You look very young, have you ever been in office before?" He didn't look up from examining the piece of folded paper. She was now rethinking the purple bow she had tied into her low ponytail and her lack of eyeliner.

"Well, I'm a recent college graduate. I'm fairly new to politics, but I feel like I am still qualified for this position—"

"Why?" the man looked up and he shifted to the side. She got a peek into his home, it was small and modest, with a well-worn khaki armchair and a chunky oak coffee table that took up the majority of the living room. On the kitchen counter, she saw that oh-so familiar Owenz pasta, with its mustard box and burnt orange font: the Dinali pasta tax.

"I am very knowledgeable on our current political climate." She straightened up, feeling confidence rev in her stomach. "I'm passionate about this specific election cycle because it's personal for me." The man leaned into the doorframe, his hair moving swiftly. She explained her father's situation. "Why do other parties, specifically members from the Beldan Sour Cream ™ Party, feel the need to punish faithful employees? Old Yolk City is known for our pasta production, and yes the money raised from these tax increases on local goods could lead to more social programs, but it would be doing more harm than good." The old man's face scrunched up into a small smile.

"Huh, okay. What did you say your name was? Um, Jane...Whoopersmith? A little unconventional, eh? I've been a loyal member of the Beldan party since I was in high school. Did the RPS set you up to this? ...This walking around thing?" He swirled his finger around in the air. Beads of sweat raced down her back. She had said too much.

"No, it was my idea. I felt like no one was paying attention to me. So, I thought I should go out and interact." Her posture began to falter.

"Hmm, I like that Jane. You're mixing things up. But this city works in a certain way. It works well. I don't know if some things need to change."

"There's nothing you're dissatisfied about within the Beldan Sour CreamTM Party?" She wasn't sure why she was still pushing. She wasn't mad. He did listen to her, but an urge of competition began building in her toes. He laughed, or more so did one of those mono-syllabic exertions that came out as *hah*.

"I don't see myself switching over, if that's what you're asking. You keep saying the full name. Beldan would suffice, ya know."

"I'm just saying the technical name. The Beldan Sour Cream ™ company does contribute a lot of money to the party. Isn't it strange that they want to attack other local businesses?" said Jane.

"Yeah I don't love that part of the party. When they auctioned off their name...I knew that was a turn in the wrong direction." He looked down at the pamphlet. Which he'd begun tearing away at one of the corners.

"Anyway, thank you for speaking with me, sir." She would count this interaction as a win. She needed something to propel her to the next house. Maybe this wasn't hopeless.

"I'll talk to just about anyone, but I give you props, Jane. Who's running against you?"

"Deppy Silverjaw." The old man made a face.

"Those Silverjaws are everywhere. I'm gonna give this to my daughter. She'd be interested, she's always talking about politics." He waved the pamphlet back and forth. "I hope to see you around, Jane."

***

Within the next few days, word began to spread about Jane after a newspaper article for the *Old Yolk Times* did a piece about her. She went door-to-door with every free minute she had. She was actually having some fruitful conversations. It started off by multiple people calling in to complain about her being a nuisance in the neighborhood, but the prominent journalist, Sydney Potcott must have thought it was interesting and called Jane for an interview about her going door-to- door. She began to get hordes of emails and phone calls and RPS reached out to her and officially endorsed her as a part of their party. Some of the messages pledged their vote. Others just spewed insults. One of her favorites was, "You look like a child, and children shouldn't be allowed to run for a position like this." This made her chuckle because the Beldan Party had endorsed an initiative to lower the eligible ages for all offices to 12, so one of the hotshots of the party could have his son run to get out of his Civics class.

One particular day, when Jane was left in charge of closing down the shop, someone walked in fifteen minutes before closing.

"Just so you know, we're closing soon, but let me know if I can help you with anything," she said, her back to the door. She dusted the front window display which consisted of a delicate life-size origami sculpture of an alligator, along the sides of the windows hung delicate strands of colorful paper beads that her co-worker made.

"Hi Jane, I don't believe we've formally met." He walked over towards her, his limbs so long and gangly, it looked like they got stuck in a taffy puller. It was Deppy Silverjaw. He was wearing a sleek leather jacket and straight blond hair that brushed his ears.

"Oh, Deppy, hey." She set down her duster on the front counter. She didn't mean to sound so casual around her professional opponent, but she didn't expect it to be him. She thought that it was going to be the man who owned the stone tablet warehouse down the street, that usually came in to argue which was more sustainable. His name was Arthur.

"Interesting place to work." Deppy picked up a ream of lined paper.

"What do you want?"

"It's fun and all that this is turning into a real race, but I just need to get my foot in the door. You know that you can't do anything in this position right?" He leaned against a shelf that held purple origami paper, leaving one of the pages creased.

"Oh, I'm sorry that you thought this was just going to be another easy election. I don't think there's anything we can do to change that now. Did you know that our current mayor started off as an Assistant [2] City Manager? I have ideas, I'll get stuff done." She didn't know where this edge came from. Ever since the article was published, she had been focusing more and more time on her campaign. She was still doing everything herself, although she was trying to convince Kevin to help her. More people had been willing to speak to her, some even inviting her in for some warm milk or a salami sandwich. However, those who didn't want to talk to her made it much more apparent: with slammed doors and poisonous looks. Some of the more extreme citizens started distributing signs to put in their front lawn that said, "No Politicians Allowed Here" or "Jane Go Away". At least those signs helped save her some time.

"I just don't get why you care. *You* don't have to be a politician," said Deppy, like a pouting child.

"You don't either?" She was confused by this whole interaction. She assumed that she was supposed to be intimidated by his presence, instead her mind wandered to the new episode of *Celebrity Deep-Sea Fishing* that aired the previous night.

"Yeah, I do. What else would I remotely be qualified in doing?" He looked around as if asking the items on the shelves for guidance.

"Why are you worried about the financial implications of the animal healthcare programs?"

"What are you talking about?" His face went blank, his charming smile ironed out.

"You've never heard of it. So, how are you *qualified* exactly? Why should you get this position?" She wasn't wearing heels, but she suddenly felt taller than him.

"We don't need to know all of those silly details." His body collapsed like a windswept tree.

"Why did you come here? To try to get me to drop out? You're not that scary, Deppy."

"No not at all. I just wanted to talk." He looked down at his pointed leather boots.

"We're now closed, so I have to ask you to leave," Jane said, glancing at her watch. Deppy hesitated.

"Do you think my dad gave me the choice to run?" His voice dropped in register, almost to a whisper. He shifted his eyes down, almost self-conscious.

"You're an adult, you don't have to listen to whatever your dad tells you!" Jane chuckled.

The Silverjaws were scary people, with their pointy cheekbones and the clouds of ego that perfumed their necks, but they could only do so much.

"Jane." Deppy eyes expanded like sponges. "You know nothing about politics." He shook his head and left.

The next morning, the soundbites were everywhere. She got a call from her mom, who was panicking. Her parents had continued to be supportive. Her mom would occasionally drop off sandwiches on her way to work. They were excited about the newspaper articles and the attention. Although, Jane could sense that the hostility from the Beldan members worried them. Usually no one cared about this election, or really any election, for that matter. However, on her way to campaign that morning, her and Deppy's names were fluttering around. Kevin even texted Jane to tell her that his Human Situations teacher brought it up at the start of class that morning.

Most of the soundbites weren't even direct quotes, they were so obviously cut together haphazardly. Her tone of voice and volume changed with each word: "You should leave in the first place", "You should drop out", "I don't care". One wasn't even a grammatical sentence: "I try intimidate you". Yet, from the looks of her emails, people were believing them. One of the emails was from Channel 2.5 asking for an interview for later that day. She needed to get ahead of this. She wasn't going to let Deppy benefit from this, even though she knew it wasn't his idea.

Before she could fully prepare herself, she was having a live conversation with Suzanna Taiport, an anchor that she had watched every morning in high school. Jane felt like she had swallowed some batteries and hoped she hadn't made a mistake.

"So, Jane Whoopersmith, there were some soundbites that were released this morning that were a little confusing in relation to your race. You're running for Assistant [2] City Manager, correct?"

"Yes, Suzanna, I had a conversation with Deppy Silverjaw last night and I was not aware that I was being recorded. I didn't say anything that I regret. However, some of my words were spliced together to make me come across as attacking and vindictive. I just wanted to clear this up." Jane paused. "I would also like to take this time to propose a debate between the candidates running for this position so the people can hear our own words." Suzanna's face stretched back momentarily; she had not been briefed about this announcement, and neither had Jane because the notion just crossed her mind.

The next day, Sydney Protcott, the same journalist who did the initial article introducing Jane to Old Yolk City, contacted her again for a follow up to specifically talk about the debate she proposed. They met up at one of Old Yolk City's premiere artisan water shops, which was right outside of the *Old Yolk Times* building. They sat outside on the patio, and it was almost completely dark even though it was not even four in the afternoon.

"Deppy hasn't responded," Jane said.

"That's not surprising. His father is probably figuring out a way to control the situation, he's probably wishing that he organized it. However, if you want to name a time and place, this article could serve as a further call to action." Sydney leaned back against her chair, her glasses slipping down her small nose.

"Yeah, you're right. I just don't know if I should keep doing these things. I feel like everyone is so annoyed with me," said Jane. After the words left her mouth, she remembered that this wasn't a therapy session, even though Sydney does look like a passable therapist. She sipped her warm plum water, shutting herself up.

"People are excited about you. I mean, when my dad told me what you were doing, I knew I had to write an article. Especially since my dad has been a long time Beldan voter. I'm surprised he even talked to you."

"I talked to your dad?"

"Yeah he's over on Coast Street? He's older, short white hair?" Sydney waved her hand over her head.

"He was the first person to talk to me." She paused. "Okay. Let's do it. I'm calling for a debate between all of the Assistant2 City Manager candidates at this year's Duck-Run-About-Jamboree."

The day before the Jamboree, Deppy visited Jane at work again, this time it was minutes after the shop opened.

"Hi, Deppy. Are you recording me again?" Jane didn't look up from opening a new shipment of hibiscus-colored tissue paper.

"No, don't worry. Stunts like that only really work once. Although, you didn't even take that hard of a hit. My dad didn't see that coming and he's been in this game for a while." His elongated legs strode down each individual aisle. He touched and messed with all of the merchandise.

"I can't believe your dad is controlling your every move. Why do they even care?" She walked from behind the counter to stand in front of Deppy who was flipping through a stack of recycled paper.

"You're doing okay, I guess...They don't want someone with some degree of persuasion in city council." He looked at her as if she started growing an elephant trunk in the middle of her face.

"Why are you telling me this? I don't see how this benefits you," Jane said. He was wearing the same leather jacket as before and he looked tired.

"I'm telling you—because you don't know what you're doing. You don't want to get involved," his voice cracked. He was a worse actor than Richard Dapper, who was the famous soap opera star for the Northbound C bus. Each bus line had a different daily soap opera that aired on a loop for 24 hours. There was a whole subculture of people that spent all day riding and watching the different episodes. Richard Dapper was charming and handsome, but the least convincing cowboy on *Rein Me In*.

"You're not really good at this whole intimidation thing. You were much more threatening from afar, hidden behind the rumors."

"Oh, c'mon none of those are true. People here need more sunlight, they're so bored they draw up lies about a teenager. I mean...I stole one car, and I occasionally buy fancy mints, but we all have vices, don't we?" He crossed his arms, and his leather arms squeaked pathetically.

"Tell your dad to help you with some talking points for tomorrow," Jane said, tying her work apron around her waist.

"I'll pass that message along." Deppy had a playful smirk on his face, he leaned against the front counter. "I don't believe you're doing this just to be the perfect daughter and save your dad's job."

"Excuse me?" Where were these snide comments coming from? What right did he have? She was enjoying this exchange, in a sadistic way. She liked the debate and the back and forth.

Maybe he had a point. "Okay. It isn't my only motivation anymore. So what? Maybe I'm good at this political thing?"

"Yeah, that's what worries us. You are good at it. It's even worse that you know it. I have no chance." Deppy threw up his hands.

"Show up to the debate, test me. You're not an idiot." Jane straightened up a stack of books on the front table. She wasn't entirely sure if she believed her comment.

"Oh, thanks for your confidence in me," Deppy said, huffing. A customer walked in the door. "I'll humiliate myself if I show up or not." The customer waved at Jane for assistance with one of the rolls of wrapping paper that was out of her reach. Deppy left the store without saying any more.

The Duck-Run-About-Jamboree was an annual tradition. Duck racing used to be a big deal for the wealthy in Old Yolk City, but now it was a bit of a kitschy event that everyone got really into. Raoul was the leading champion from the past few years: a picture-perfect Mallard. The race took place every Autumn and this year was the 76th anniversary. It was complete with rides, face painting and food, as well as the famous 5-legged race that involved three people, one of whom could only use one leg. Everyone in town went. It was so big that it took over literally the entire city.

There was no response from Deppy, even after their talk. The debate would take place in the morning. Some of the organizers weren't thrilled about this festival turning political. There was buzz, however, so the festival gave them 45 minutes on the main stage. Trucker's Jug Band and Friends was going on after them, so Jane expected a good turnout, because no one could draw a crowd like Trucker.

On Saturday morning, Jane put on a fitted eggplant dress, but added a blazer to make her look more official. She wore her tallest heels, red patent-leather stilettos. She showed up with her parents and Kevin. They arrived and got some cinnamon nuts and a Traditional Duck, a puff cherry pastry decorated to look like Raoul. They munched on their treats at a yellow-painted picnic table. The annual raccoon puppet show was going on at the smaller stage, and they could hear the kids' laughter even though they were yards away. Kevin was helping Jane fold some last-minute pamphlets; he and their parents were going to hand them out while Jane was on stage. They were all wearing large buttons and homemade t-shirts that her mom had made with fabric paint.

Then it was time for the debate. With still no word from Deppy, it was just Jane on stage with an empty podium to her left. Suzanna Taiport was the moderator. The questions were all easy and expected. There was a decent crowd forming and they were listening, and she recognized some faces that she met going door-to-door. There was a lady upfront named Susan that was the president of the Old Yolk Carnivore Society that had sent her away with some delicious jerky.

"We would have money for all of these programs if we just got rid of some of the many unnecessary elements in our local government. There are so many inefficient departments! We can find the money." Jane's comment was met with much positive hollering.

As Jane was explaining her views for the millionth time, Deppy stepped on stage to a round of applause. He was wearing a charcoal suit, black dress shoes, his hair was still shaggy, and he wasn't wearing a tie.

"Sorry for my late arrival, I was helping set up the duck race. This is such an important tradition in our town, and I've helped and volunteered ever since I could walk," Deppy said, flashing a smile and waving at the audience as if they were old friends, with much applause.

"Thanks for showing up, Deppy. Jane was in the middle of her thoughts," Suzanna said.

"I think I would like to hear about Deppy's opinion on the matter. I'm kind of tired of hearing my own voice," the crowd chuckled along with her. "I bet he has an interesting take, especially since he loves tradition." Jane beamed at Deppy. She didn't think he was going to show up. She sensed an element of sabotage. She didn't trust him, she weirdly felt bad for him. Even though he had everything in the world that a person could need.

"Good idea! So, Deppy what do you think will happen to the infrastructure of our pet stores if we open up the market to weasels?" Suzanna adjusted her glasses. Deppy gripped the sides of his podium, denting them since they were just made out of cardboard— there was no time to get fancy ones.

"Why shouldn't we have weasels? I think our pet stores can handle it. I love weasels, my ex- girlfriend Tamera had one and it wore a cute sweater." He ran his fingers through his hair. There were some mutters from the audience.

"So, you're changing your position regarding weasels? Beldans are against this inclusion."

The crowd talked amongst one another. Deppy pulled out a notecard from his pocket and fumbled with it. Even though Jane wanted this win more than anything, more than that curatorial job, she hated seeing Deppy like this.

"Suzanna, give Deppy a new question. I don't think he's had much experience on a stage. He's probably a little nervous," Jane said. Suzanna nodded and asked him a question about his prospective goals with this position. Deppy and Jane locked eyes, he shook his head a little but grinned. She had done exactly what he wanted her to.

"Thanks for giving me a softball, but I don't really care about this position. I've gotta be honest. As a Silverjaw, I'm supposed to like this world, but I don't and frankly I would be horrible at it. However, my lovely candidate, Jane, has made me push away these apprehensions. She has made me want to do better. I think we can do more. The ways of Old Yolk City are ancient and outdated. I'm willing to give it a shot from a new perspective. Don't vote for me because I'm a Silverjaw. Vote for me because I'm Deppy." He smirked as if he had already won. Seconds later, two men in similar looking shirts carried out a large banner in bright green font that only had the word 'Deppy' multiple times. The two men held the sign with a blank stare. She recognized one of them as one of the other Silverjaw boys. Jane stifled a laugh at her podium, but there were hoots and whooping from the crowd.

After the debate at the Jamboree, there was still two weeks left in the race. Jane continued her intense door-to-door method. Deppy tried to copy her and failed. Deppy's father tried to run his campaign, but kept referring to the wrong child, so people were confused on who to vote for. There were bombardments of radio ads and billboards. He even paid for a portrait of Deppy to be hung over the Overmert Toothbrush sculpture that stood in the middle of Toonsy Park, which was a staple for tourists to take a picture with.

Jane won the race along with a lot of other Rock, Paper, Scissors candidates. It was a close one, though. Some thought it was rigged. Others blamed the large outbreak of Bird Snot (a horrible virus in which the infected uncontrollably leaks from their nose) right before the election, which kept some people from going out to vote. Jane liked to think that she was the one that drew them out, but she wasn't entirely sure. She was in the RPS offices, with her family and the other people running, when it was officially announced. There were plastic cups of sparkling apricot juice and her parents beamed, shaking hands with everyone in the office. Jane's father kept snapping photos every few seconds on his ancient digital camera and kissing her on the forehead. She just hoped that she could actually save his job. Jane wore a new purple pantsuit that her mother had gifted her that morning. She saw the buzzing faces of the newly elected officials around her, all antsy to get started.

**

Office of the Major
City of Old Yolk

Ms. Jane Whoopersmith,

 I hope this letter finds you well. It was exciting seeing such a bright young woman sworn in this week. We were all surprised by you. I hope you had a good week here, I had heard your name a lot. However, I'm sorry to send such frightful news your way and I apologize this couldn't have been in person. I liked your idea in the debate at the Duck Jamboree about cutting the fat of the local government. I want to fund all of these programs without hurting our citizens more, and I think this is a good way to do that. So, I regret to inform you that your position as Assistant [2] *City Manager will be cut and starting Monday it will no longer be a position in Old Yolk City.*
Best,

Toddlin Ruppers

***

A few weeks later, Jane collected her campaign materials, all with the familiar lilac details, however, this time for her mayoral run. She had a few hours before work to do some door-to-doors. Kevin was going to help her out for some of it, he was going to start at the opposite end of the street. Jane slipped on her black sneakers, the same ones from her first campaign, but quickly realized that she could feel the cold wood floor under her heels. She peeked underneath and saw the holes in both of her shoes.

Flypaper
By Glen Armstrong

In the hearts of those sick people.
My home is made over.
As a sheet of flypaper.
With border walls.
It's all call and no response.
These days.
From their corner office windows.
I am a fly with shit.
In my furry legs.
I am the bagman with egg.

Shell stuck to the windbreaker.
Saint Vincent gave me.
In my pockets.
A dead man prevails.
In the takeout containers.
Of the rich and famous.
In their packages from Amazon.
Some fantasy world arrives.
While they fail to piece it together.
It's getting sticky outside.

Flyswatter
By Glen Armstrong

Maybe a whispering soul.
Stabs at the air.
Around my head like a bumblebee.
Needing to tell me.
A joke or a warning or a secret.
About walking and the envy it stirs.
Up in the spirit world.
Maybe an actual bumblebee.
Positions itself near my ear.
Like a whispering soul.

Already drenched in pollen and down.
To clown.
Maybe not.
Gail from down the street.
Knocks at the door.
I have her.
In for instant coffee and pocket.
Creamers procured from the diner.
She thinks this rotten world.
Is just a test for the next.

Poem I Hid Inside Your Book and Then on Second Thought Retrieved
By Indigo Erlenborn

You thunder, silver-tongued
about your alien planet
like a junkyard guard dog,

dislodge thick snarls from your throat.

Taste the rusted air for fear.

I do not know the climate here.
I do not care to-

this wasteland is too crowded as it is,
there is no place for me to rest
among all these damn mirrors that reek of
restlessness and
wine.

If only I could close my eyes
and let the ancient howl of your spirit's storm
engulf me,

force me to remember
I must breathe.

But I do not know the climate here.

I do not care to.

Nettle Boys
By Indigo Erlenborn

Withered and acrid
are these stinging-nettle boys.

Their gnawing, blackened sneers cuff
my ankles in red lace
and my mother, pitiless, shrugs the blood away
having clearly given up on my
wearing shoes.

I ran by night,
from what I did
not know.

By that first pillowing of dawn I found
my legs etched raw,
as if by dying captive men
that count the days on walls
of tide-choked caves,

and prison cells
and on the ribs of tombs

when one gets mixed up in that unsavory business
of being buried alive.

They scored my skin to play a round
of tic-tac-toe to pass the idle time
they stole from me

and still

I sing only

of their thorns.

Einstein's Beauty Built the Bomb
By feeble organs

Courtesy of Collins Dictionary:
"If someone wrings their hands,
they hold them together and twist and turn them,
usually because they are very worried or upset about something.
You can also say
that someone is wringing their hands
when they are expressing sorrow that a situation
is so bad
but are saying they are unable to change it."
There you are,
wringing your hands
 giddy with anticipation.
I haven't seen you since college
when you slept on the mattresses we fished from a dumpster,
claiming we had a couch now.
Steve sprayed it with Febreze
because even though we wanted to be young and free, Steve
and me
knew it was a little gross.

You liked gross.
I'd learn years later that you enjoy videos of people popping blisters
and I didn't really judge
or if I did
I liked it about you: to be so open
and young and free.
One day you'll tell me about the underworld,
South Philadelphia, trafficking H and watching anime.
We told you not to worry,
we Febrezed your bed
and clothed it with jersey sheets.

You laughed;
"If there is one thing I'm racist against," your face shifts awry,
"it's microbes."
I knew I liked you then.

You hadn't eaten in days,
choosing weed over food like some sort of paradox
internalizing a resistance to bad jokes and expectations.
Sitting in a picnic chair,
 surrounded by your fellow adoring fans
of Penn State Football,
you'd teach these plebs
 about Iran–Contra.
Nothing about you makes sense.

There you are,

wringing your hands
looking up to me sitting at a high table.
You were dressed how you always dressed;
 I was squirming in formal wear,
in the party of honor on Steve's wedding day.

That wry smile turned up both cheeks today.
You can't wait to get home
and self-destruct.
I'd think back to you sitting on that gross ass couch
sharing your soul in the form of song,
a new shared love of Huggable Dust,
"What a nightmare to love" repeating endlessly.
I'd talk about Neutral Milk Hotel like I do every day,
but you had never heard of them.

You'd tell me later
you knew you liked me then.

I wonder what it felt like
looking up to me
wringing your hands like that.
The day is done with deli meats and supermarket sales
and you are looking forward to a bubble bath in the black tar.

There will come a day
when we reconnect
from different states,
both bottoming out.
Still not on a level plane.

I lost my only love, my friends, and self-respect;
you lost just about everything but your car.
You'd tell me tales from the driver's seat --
Life in Vermont
and all these fucking artists
vying for their next big break.
You held a mirror with these judgements.
I wondered why you liked me.
I wondered if I liked myself.

I just want to be done with this poem.
I don't like thinking about these things.

But I keep coming back to you.

It Helps
By feeble organs

It helps to think of humans as stick figures.
Nothing solid but a frame.
A pipe bent from end to end,
consuming lead
put there by some self-described demigod
choosing who and what exists.
It helps to think of humans this way.
Pretty much a waste of space.
Sometimes in motion,
usually standing still.
A hope of an idea
unblossomed.
Lacking color,
undifferentiated,
plain,
dull.
These figures draw me closer
and then push me away
as if asking me to erase myself.
Do not forget,
I am built of blood.
I could show it to you,
I really could.
But it's better to keep to myself.

THE BISHOP SAID TO THE ACTRESS
By J.E.A. Wallace

The words on the protest signs run in the rain
They resemble the mixed-up faces
Of the furiously implacable holding them

And above
Looking down
On their squeezed and angry wriggling

The Archbishop
Of a city to the north
That burned all the way down to its catacombs

Last week? Last month?

                                     Time has felt strange to him lately

Like trying to remember why you're in the wrong room

She is not that far away
The woman he came here to what?
Warn? Rescue? Endanger?

He is after all a man
In charge of the spiritual welfare
Of a city that just set itself on fire

Not exactly a lucky charm then
But can he stay away from her?
His decisions recently leave much to be desired

Her theatre is close
But also close to the ground
Ground perpetually covered with these people

Who'd love to see his like
Rethink their previous certainty
About the number and position of their limbs

He picks up the phone
And she answers tearfully
He changes his mind and says 'Don't leave'

ENCUMBRANCE
By Joe Baumann

When I saw Mara at the end of school, her cummerbund was red. I told her that our mother would be angry.

"Yea. And it's all talk." Mara turned right when we walked out of the building, away from the buses and cars, not just because we walked home but because she liked to smoke a surreptitious cigarette from one of the packs her boyfriend bought for her, himself not old enough to buy them but in possession of a good enough fake ID to get past the sleepy, pimply college dropout that worked at the nearby gas station.

Mara shoved ahead of me. Even though we were twins, she loomed larger than me, our classmates, and some of the teachers. Word on the street was that even the gym teacher didn't cross her, letting Mara sit on the bleachers while her classmates played bombardment or ran the mile. The only person capable of instilling even the remotest glimmer of fear in my sister's stony eyes was our mother, who had sat us both down when we were eleven years old and told us that we were, in no uncertain terms, not to allow our cummerbunds to change from pink to red before we were sixteen.

"When you get there, all bets are off. Fine. But until then, no. Absolutely not. Understand me?"

I had nodded vigorously, my feet dangling from the couch. Mara, already willow tree tall, stared at my mother, who glared back. After a long silence, the fire of my mother's mascaraed eyes burning the atmosphere around her head, Mara finally nodded too.

But then, on that blustery March afternoon during the final months of our sophomore year of high school, she slunk out of the building, her cummerbund a dark, bloody red. I blurted out, "What happened?" before I could stop myself. She blinked at me and told me that Rodney Piper, the superstar quarterback of the football team, had kissed her on the lips after English, saying it as if it was nothing more than another detail of her day, like what a teacher said or which idiot boy from math class farted loud enough for people to start laughing.

I looked down at my own cummerbund, still an unblemished Easter pink. A lot of kids our age had new colors; there had been a minor uproar when Kelly Garfield walked in one Monday during seventh grade and hers was already yellow. She sat at her desk, not making eye contact with our teacher, Mrs. Figgins, who pretended nothing was amiss and told us to be quiet so she could start science class. But no one listened to her. She was trying to get us to understand the concept of sublimation, when a solid goes straight to a gaseous state without becoming a liquid in between. I tried to imagine what it must have been like for Kelly Garfield, leaping straight from pink to yellow, barging right past first-kiss red and, well, whatever would happen at orange. My face warmed when my thoughts started to wander. I sat right behind Kelly, and I stared at the back of her neck all of class, a tangle of long hairs sweeping toward her shirt collar. I wondered if someone had touched her there, as a starting point, before moving into territory I knew about but felt wholly lost in.

I caught up to Mara where she stood around the side of the building. Our high school had surveillance cameras mounted on every corner, but my sister knew exactly where to stand to be hidden in their narrow slice of blind spot. She wasn't worried about teachers coming around back, because the only people who ever went there were the maintenance staff or the football coach, who, unless you were one of all-state running backs or defensive linemen, acted like you didn't exist.

Mara said nothing as she blew out smoke. I don't know when my sister started on cigarettes, but it was sometime in the eighth grade. She would suck down one, exhaling away from me, and then pop two sticks of Juicyfruit before adjusting her backpack and taking off for home. Today she acted no different.

For all my sister's disdain for our parents' rules, she constantly guffawed at how disgusting our classmates were, as though she was above them all, belonging instead in college already. It's true that she was smart and seemed to have unfurled the world's secrets in a way that the other fifteen-year-olds had not. She aced tests without studying, and when she did her homework she zoomed through and still got perfect scores, rolling her eyes and huffing the questions out loud with annoyed irony. When she had to read *Where the Red Fern Grows* in fifth grade, she kept throwing the book across the room, announcing before she was finished that she knew the damn dogs would die. But Rodney Piper was sandy-haired and muscular, and he cracked jokes that were mostly at his own expense, and everyone knew that, when it wasn't football season, he played cards with seniors at the assisted-living facility down the street from school. His smile was blazing and magazine worthy.

We stalked home in silence. Our house's yard backed up against the upper lip of a hill behind the football field. Mara climbed the steep embankment and then leapt over our chain-link fence without breaking her stride. She had a much easier time with this not only because she was taller than me but she also left her textbooks in her locker most of the time, only bringing home the worksheets she had to fill out for the next day, so her bag was like an empty paper sack on her shoulders. When I reached the fence I dangled my bag to the ground on the other side, careful to lower it as slowly as I could so it didn't get streaked with too much muck, and then dug one foot into the diamond holes in the fence and launched myself over with as much grace—and clearance—as I could muster, but I still felt my legs scrape against the bar at the top and I tumbled into the grass.

When I finally got inside, my heart was pounding. I stepped through the sliding door into the kitchen and stood still, listening for sounds. Our mother worked from home three days a week, though I always managed to forget which ones and had to take stock upon arrival to sort out whether she was there or not. I could hear Mara already pounding around in her bedroom, which was right above the kitchen; she clomped so hard that I was sure that one of these days her feet would burst right through the floor, dangling above the butcher block and Wusthof knife set. But I heard nothing, no screaming from our mother or her own Espadrilled feet slamming on the Berber carpet or clomping up or down the stairs.

Her office was empty, the glass-topped desk scattered with paperwork. Our mother sold commercial real estate, disinclined to work with what she called "Hippy Dippy Mary Annes" who didn't realize that they couldn't qualify for the mortgage it would take to buy a four-bedroom house in a good school district on a freelance ballet dancer's salary. She cold-called businesses small and large, had her pulse on where a new deli or flower shop would go boom versus bust. She knew how to sweet talk men in floral ties, their pot bellies pulled back over their too-tightly-belted pants, how to flirt with them over martinis and raw steaks in low-lit restaurants.

I listened for Mara's footsteps. I heard the squeal of her bed and then nothing, and I imagined her lying there, staring down at the fabric of her cummerbund. Ours were identical, four inches wide, mine reaching from my hip bones up to my belly button, the fabric creasing and denting whenever I sat down and making me feel bloated, fat. Mara's, somehow, managed to never inflate like a life preserver around her waist, leaving her eternally slim and sultry. I wasn't surprised that Rodney Piper wanted to kiss her or that she had a boyfriend too old for her who was willing, still, to wait to so much as plant his lips on hers. Everyone wanted Mara.

I pulled a baggie of deli turkey from the fridge and heaped a few tissue paper-thin slices on a plate. I poured myself a glass of milk and stalked up the stairs, pausing at Mara's door but could hear nothing inside. When our parents were home, she blasted obnoxious pop music at absurd volumes, so high my teeth vibrated. Neither my mother nor father screamed for her to turn it down because they'd figured out that this was exactly what she wanted, digging under their skin as much as she could. They simply bought packages of cheap earplugs and shoved them in when she decided to be noisy, unless my mother had an important phone call, in which case she simply barreled into my sister's room without knocking and turned off the music, which was the onlytime Mara wouldn't immediately turn it back on, knowing that my mother might then take her computer speakers away, tossing them into the garbage can like she did when we were ten and Mara didn't believe our mother was being serious when she threatened to do just that.

I listened for maybe two minutes before I shuffled past her door to my own, separated by an entrance to our shared bathroom. I sat on my bed and ate my turkey one small hunk at a time, taking tiny sips of milk between bites. The chill hurt my teeth, but I welcomed it. I looked down at my cummerbund, its pink the same as the wilty, embarrassed color of my cheeks that I could never quite get to go away.

*

Our mother howled. She slammed everything down on the dining room table: utensils, plates, drinking glasses, the trough with the roast she reheated from Whole Foods. Our father blinked and watched, but neither said a word. She glared at Mara but didn't threaten, which only made the stink of tension increase. I tried to eat, but my jaw didn't want to work. My throat clogged around every chewed-up ball of food I attempted to swallow. Mara pretended to be blithely unaware, but I caught her leaning back with extra bend in her back so the red cummerbund pushed forward. Our parents didn't have them; they hadn't existed when they were born, and if you didn't have them engaged from the very beginning they didn't work. The meal ended abruptly the second my mother had sucked down the last of her glass of wine—she and my father each drank one serving of Beaujolais at every evening meal, and that was all the alcohol I ever saw them consume—and she started clearing everything away, even though Mara and my father were still eating. When their plates vanished, they said nothing. I excused myself and scuttled upstairs to try to focus on *Lord of the Flies.*

The mounting minutes of no eruption were terrible. My jaw ached, I was clenching my teeth so hard; my ears prickled, waiting to hear the noise of a fight, but none came. A hearty wind blustered all night, creaking the frame and whipping at the glass of my bedroom window. At some point, someone turned on a television, a faint buzz of noise that extinguished itself when the volume was lowered. I listened for the sound of my sister blaring her music, but nothing came. Eventually I turned off my overhead light and laid in bed, one hand on my cummerbund, the other on my chest, and I tried to feel something connecting the two.

*

I, too, wanted Rodney Piper to kiss me. I, too, wanted to have Mara's boyfriend, a kid in eleventh grade who had given himself a bicep tattoo when he was thirteen and had somehow managed not to infect himself with staph or hepatitis. I saw him once, when I was out riding my bike in lieu of anything else to do, and spotted Mara leaning into the cab of a mangy pickup truck. I was far down the street but could see his pale beauty, the tendrils of his black hair that drizzled down his forehead like seaweed. When his arm reached out toward my sister's face, I could see the plump white of well-formed muscle. He didn't kiss Mara then, or ever, to my knowledge. The cummerbunds didn't lie. It wasn't until a month later that hers changed from its pure pink to ravaged red. That was the descriptor so many adults used: ravaged, as if a single kiss was the worst thing in the world that could happen. Sometimes I touched my fingers to my lips at night, convinced that to have someone else's there would, instead, be the best, the brightest, the most righteous thing that could happen.

*

Because my parents said nothing about her cummerbund's change, Mara pushed her luck: two days later, she walked out of school and it was orange. I had just failed a geopolitics test, and my brain was on the fritz. I'd forgotten the arrangement of the Middle East on a map, mismanaging Iraq, Iran, Kuwait, and Yemen.

"What happened?" I said.

"Wouldn't you like to know." She kept walking around the side of the school as usual. This time, though, she didn't stop for a secret cigarette.

My heart was pounding. I didn't want to explain my terrible test performance to my parents, nor did I wish to be present when they saw what had become of my sister's cummerbund. Everything in me ached on different frequencies, like my body was an orchestra warming up but each instrument was playing different scales. Mara walked ahead of me, body slanting forward as she pitched up the hill toward our house. The weather had taken a warm turn and she was wearing a skirt. I watched her calf muscles twitch, her hamstrings sharpening like a violinist's bow. She leapt over the fence and left me in the lurch. I didn't feel like making the effort to jump so I decided to take the long way around. The houses on either side of ours were also fenced-in, wood planks and plastic rails making the property line look like a mismatched mouth, some teeth pristine, others rotten, others encased in braces. Four houses down I was finally able to slink through a back yard and out to the sidewalk, where I started doubling back.

I stopped: my sister's boyfriend's truck was parked three doors down from our house, facing against traffic. I recognized the basketball-sized puncture wound in the back bumper, where it looked like someone had punched the metal with a gigantic fist. The red paint was streaky and blotted with white rust. It was idling, smoke choking out of the exhaust pipe like something out of an old-timey cartoon. Then I watched my sister appear on our front porch. She started her signature, languorous walk at a diagonal across our yard. Then my sister—grizzled, angry Mara—started skipping when she was a few car lengths away from her boyfriend's truck. I heard her hands clap against the open driver's side window. She leaned in, and I could see the silhouette of her boyfriend's head cock to the side as they kissed. Mara swished around the front of the truck and hopped in the cab, and her boyfriend revved the engine before peeling down the street. She lifted her arm out the passenger-side window, raising her middle finger. At first I thought she was flipping me off, but then I realized she was aiming her ire directly at our house as she and her boyfriend sped away.

*

The atmosphere in our house was a thick syrup of rage that I could feel as soon as I pushed in through the front door. A clomp of steps echoed from its belly and my mother appeared in the foyer. She wore a body-tight black dress and heels, her hair cut in a tight bob that barely brushed her shoulders. My mother's features were sharp, bird-like. I had her nose, which angled straight down and out from her face.

"I thought you'd be Mara."

"Why?"

"She stormed out a minute ago. Where have you been?"

"Walking home from school."

"What took so long?"

"I went the long way."

My mother stared, like she had no idea what that meant. She pushed her fists against her hips.

"Well?"

"Well, what?"

"Do you know where she is?"

"No," I said.

"You're a good one, Malcolm," my mother said. "Stay that way."

Before I could say anything about her boyfriend and the truck, my mother vanished into her office.

*

When Mara didn't come back in an hour, my parents called the police. A balding detective sat down with me in the living room, alone, asking me questions. Sweat percolated on his receding hair line and his eyes were blurry behind thick glasses. I spent an hour repeating all the synonyms I knew for the words red and truck and loud. I felt a certain sting of shame when I admitted I couldn't remember the license plate, and I had to assure him, four, five, six times that I did not know the name of the person who had absconded—the detective's word—with my sister. He said her name like a hammer striking a nail, looking over the rim of his glasses at me as if it was my fault that she was gone. The police set up some kind of plan, in case a kidnapper seeking ransom called—I gulped down a guffawed laugh at the idea that my sister was being held hostage somewhere—and then they left, telling us to call if anything happened, but that, until she'd been gone for twenty-four hours, there was little they could do. My mother, buzzy with angry energy, fluttered around before holing herself up in her office.

I sat in my room, waiting to be called down to the kitchen until well after the usual appointed dinner time—6:30—and so I trotted out carefully, leaning out my doorway to listen for noises of anger or sorrow and instead felt just bowing, heavy silence. I plodded down to the kitchen and found no one. I sat down in the dining room and folded my hands on the table, as if this would muster up something.

My father appeared.

"Oh," he said. "Malcolm." My father was handsome and strong, shoulders like big tomatoes, the kind of expansive back I dreamed of one day growing into. He wore polo shirts whose sleeves showed off strong arms with enough musculature that the vein running up his flesh was pronounced. He had dreamy, wavy hair that fell over his eyes when he didn't get it cut often enough. Right now, it was swirled up like a cyclone had plucked at it.

"I was wondering about dinner."

"Dinner?"

"That thing we're usually eating right now?"

"Ah." He rubbed at the sides of his nose with a thumb and index finger. "That appears to have fallen by the wayside."

"Because of Mara."

"Yes, because of your sister."

"I'm sure she's okay. She can take care of herself."

"Say, why don't I order us a pizza?"

"We have frozen ones. They're pretty good and will be faster."

"Frozen it is."

He and I ate at the kitchen island, not bothering with plates. Grease dripped down our fingers, staining our palms, our mouths. My father chewed slowly and I had eaten three slices of
pepperoni before he finished his first one.

"You know," my father said, "carbs are actually worse for you than fats."

"Oh."

"Most people don't know that," he said, picking up another slice. "But let's not worry right now about what's good for us, how about?"

I nodded and took a fourth slice.

"Besides," he said. "You're fifteen. You've got a good metabolism."

"What's that mean?"

"It means you should eat and not worry about anything else."

I chewed another bite of pizza, which was doughy and tough like rawhide, and when I managed to tear it with my teeth it laid in my mouth heavy and indigestible.

"Can I ask something?" I said.

"Anything, champ." My father smiled, but his face was pinched and squished in with the effort. He had a good natural smile, so good that it was easy to spot the fake ones.

"Why these?" I said, gesturing toward my cummerbund.

"What do you mean?"

"Why'd it seem like a good idea for us to get them?"

He shrugged. "Everyone was getting them."

"But that isn't a reason."

My father took another bite of pizza, ruminating as he chewed. "I think we all thought it would help us know you better. Keep an eye on you. Not let you do anything really stupid. Keep us more aware of what was going on in your, um, private life."

"Those are all different reasons."

"Yes, I guess they are."

"But they don't really make sense. And it's not really a private life when it's on display like this."

He looked down at the pizza, then at my cummerbund. "You might be right," he said.

"Do you regret it?" I said, but I asked the question with my eyes down at my lap.

For a long time my father didn't answer. When I looked up his eyes were shimmery, and for a moment I had the stupid thought that they were filmed over with pizza grease. Only then did I realize my father was trying not to cry.

*

I was push-pulled from near-sleep at midnight by a familiar growl outside. When I went to the window that overlooked our front lawn, I saw Mara exiting her boyfriend's truck, which squealed as she crossed the yard. It shot down the street, brake lights illuminating mailboxes.

I pulled the door to my bedroom open as quietly as I could. The house buzzed with tense silence, ready to be broken with a hard crack. No noise came from any of the corners or crevices; the lights were all out up and down the second-floor hall, and no glow filtered up the stairs from the first floor. The front door clicked. I felt my pulse in my heels. I slipped out of my room and toward the stairs that spilled straight down to the front door.

Mara slid in through the door and clicked it shut behind her. She stood with her back pressed against it, hands splayed against the wood like starfish stuck to a sand bar. I could see the wide glint of her eyes, the dishevelment of her hair. She was sucking in shallow breaths and scanning the lower floor of the house, not bothering to look up at me. I was just another of the house's angled shadows, the gloms of broken, absorbed light that could trick one into thinking the house was haunted.

And then came an explosion of light. My mother and father appeared from either side of the stairs and engulfed my sister, my father trying to offer her hugs and support while my mother's voice was screechy and afraid.

They noticed at the same time I did that my sister's cummerbund was gone.

*

My parents threw Mara in the car and hauled her to the emergency room. When they came home, told by the doctor that she was fine, that whoever had taken off her cummerbund knew what they were doing, they sat her down at the kitchen table and interrogated her, and after that the police took a written statement from her and from me and from my mother and father and said there was little they could do if Mara wouldn't give them any names or details. She sat across from whoever asked her a question and held her body tight, hands snaked around her chest like chainmail, and stared, her jaw pulsing as she ground her teeth.

That Monday she told me as we walked home: "I just wanted the thing off, you know."

The boyfriend had not come back, so she hadn't smoked any cigarettes in several days. But her voice was husky from the screaming matches she found herself in with my mother. It was as if the removal of her cummerbund had unleashed all of her rage.

"What do you mean?"

"I didn't like that guy. Or Rodney." She shook her head and trudged forward. "I just hated the cummerbund."

"They are uncomfortable," I said, adjusting mine.

Mara shook her head. "That's not it."

"Then what?"

She stopped. We were halfway up the hill. "I don't think you'd understand."

I put my hands on my hips. "Try me."

But Mara said nothing. She shook her head, turned, and kept walking. She climbed over the fence like always, but this time she stopped and turned and held out her hands. Without a word I passed her my backpack, which she settled onto the grass next to her. Then she held out her hands again.

"Why are you helping me?"

She blinked. "Because I can."

We went inside. Our parents weren't home; a note, scribbled by our father and pinned to the refrigerator with an apple-shaped magnet, said that both he and our mother were working late tonight (she, a dinner; he, a conference downtown), and that there were leftovers in the fridge, or another frozen pizza.

"More pizza," I said, but Mara had already marched up the stairs to her bedroom. A few minutes later music thumped, but not as heavily as usual; the words sounded like I was hearing them underwater. I wasn't sure what to do with myself, so I sat down at the kitchen island and did homework, finishing geometry problems and then the French worksheet we'd been given at the last second by Mrs. Barden about the subjunctive.

When Mara appeared again, she cleared her throat to catch my attention. "Are you hungry?" she said.

"Kind of."

She decided to bake one of the pizzas.

"Listen, Malcolm," she said while we waited, the kitchen smelling like melting cheese. But then she didn't say anything else. She went to the fridge and found her almond milk and my two percent and poured us each a glass. When she set them down and scooched my milk toward me, careful to not let it spill on my homework, she said, "I didn't actually like Rodney Piper."

"You said that already."

She looked at me over her milk. "He was just phase one of the plan."

"Why are you telling me this?"

She tilted her head and blinked at me, then smiled. I saw, for the first time, sorrow on my sister's face. "Because I thought you should hear it." The oven's timer buzzed, and she pulled the pizza out, sliding it on the island between us. Then she said, "I don't think he liked me either."

"I don't believe that."

"Well," she said, leaning down to blow on the steaming pizza. "I think you should."

We sat there, waiting. Then, when the pizza was cool, we ate in long silence, leaning back from the counter and pressing our hands to our stomachs when we were done. Mara's fingers grazed her belly beneath the hem of her shirt. I let mine stain my cummerbund with grease, half a dozen little blipping, smeary circles that looked like the heads of ghosts.

"She'll be unhappy," Mara said, ticking her head toward the cummerbund.

"No unhappier than she is with you."

Mara smiled. "I think she's secretly proud of me."

"So am I," I said. "But I guess it's not a secret if I say it."

Mara's teeth were stained with sauce and grease; she looked like she'd just chased down a small animal and eviscerated it. She licked her tongue over them, but they looked the same. I wondered, then, what my sister was thinking. For some reason, I had not, until that moment, considered her the kind of person who did much thinking. She always seemed to know things, to never have to ponder, to wonder, to want. Worry was not a word I ever associated with my sister. Neither were fear or hope. Mara never hesitated. She just did. And now, here she was, stalling. Pondering.

Finally, she said: "You know, Malcolm, it's not the end of the world."

"What isn't?"

"Any of it." She pulled a paper towel from the dispenser and wiped her hands but left her face as it was, shining and slick. "Nothing our age is."

I felt a tingle at the back of my neck but didn't say anything.

"If you ever need anything, I can help."

"Even cigarettes?" I said as she left the room.

She turned and smirked at me. "Yeah," she said. "Even those."

Auto Parts
By Joel Glickman

Part I
Meditation on U.S. 2

for Jack Carpenter

Most of what I need to know
is before me on the dashboard
and some great mysteries as well:
1.5 x 1000—ergo 1500 rpms.
(Is that bad or good?) What other
wisdom lies beneath the hood?

And then there are some things
quietly pressing on the windscreen
and the doors I would rather have
no knowledge of at all, foremost
among them, the hateful pall of late
in America's air and always there.

So many souls that I knew, long gone,
who never had to see this— Jack,
for instance, who was a gentleman,
and taught with us on all white Kirkwood's
border with black Meacham Park, when I
was still out driving blind in my own dark.

He was the age that I am now. I can hear
his laughter yet, so kind and soft, and which
burst forth so often. He drove a little red
MG, maybe a Porsche, and, when his heart
gave out on Highway 40, he had the decency
to pull off the road and park before he died.

Most of what I know has come so slow
and in such hard-won stages. I have left,
inside my head, just enough capacity
to understand the speed and fuel gauges.

12/26/19

Auto Parts
By Joel Glickman

Part II
An OK Morning at the Ashland Ford Garage

I never mind waiting here
while they fix my minivan.
I write and eat their popcorn,
which is matchless in Ashland.

This time it is a bearing
which disabled a sensor
and the cruise-control system,
all still under warranty,

to ease my pain, and, oh yes,
the U.S.A. just took out
an Iranian hero,
in retribution, and I'm

waiting for the other shoe
to drop on that bone-headed,
bumbling piece of statesmanship.
Certainly not here or now,

but somewhere, someone will pay
a high price for my nice
day,
and those folks will never know
my good fortune is to blame.

1/3/20

Rain
By Jonel Abellanosa

This dawn brings something different,
like a hollow bone timbre. Mist spreads
to the glow in my lungs. Warmth
becomes bed. Petrichor of leaves
as I imagine rainwater to be the IV fluid,
looking at the secondary tubing,
Luer taper making voices tempt.
Distracting my selves, closing eyes
to the pitter-patter, I transcribe
the roof's speech, my mind
a palimpsest, insight a pen with ink
drying. Water leaving my eyes.

Turn

By Jonel Abellanosa

I walk to also listen, rectangle
our neighborhood, early sunlight
touching my face half the way.
Marking time with the trees
that have memorized my steps,
I follow the predetermined pathway.
I've self-conditioned to feel my pineal
gland hum and glow, each time I see
the pinecone, just before my footsteps
arc rightward at one of the four points.
I become an echo of myself minutes ago.
Each step brings me echo to echo,
like sounds of the piccolo,
each new pathway the same.

Fallow
By Kate Alsbury

Begin in rugged mountains
that stand against the darkened tide
soft-rot unnoticed
swathed in fresh white snow

Silent in the musty gloom
skeletons—
   to dust
that once fed the county wide
  coppery lustre;
    corroded green
dead—
   but not at peace

Of promises promised
long forgotten
towns whose faces shine with broken glass
and peeling paint
invisible to most
unknown love and terror
that resides

pinpricks
—nothing more
tired wasted souls
whose highest wish:
Sire those Truths of Old
and Revolt!

Not so.

Grassy fields
turned asphalt grey,
filled to bustle for a day
then stand abandoned in their fame—

   tombs awaiting their morose prey
   the haunts of fortune remain;

Remember those golden days,
That piety can will away

Resurrect those dreams now pallor,
Patience for imprudence sours.

THE LONG WAY HOME
By Kate Alsbury

Sound blisters. Daisy woke to a fountain of barely tempered voices bubbling up from across the hall. The slowest kind of crescendo, drowning the sound of young birds chortling over the last of their breakfast. Nothing unusual about this morning.

She squinted as lines of blurry red LEDs snapped into place.

6:00 a.m.
6:08 a.m.
6:30 a.m.

"It really is time to get up now," she whispered to herself.

Still dreamy, she wrapped the blanket tightly around her shoulders, feet searching in vain for slippers that had fallen apart last week. She wiggled her toes playfully over a line of ants marching from an invisible place behind peeling wallpaper (which gave everything a much more sinister air than it deserved), to unconquered lands under the dresser.

The room was small, the smallest in the house. There were only four of them—making up a little shack at the edge of a nothing much town, populated by nothing much people. It sat in the middle of a now, mostly uninhabited street. The best of the neighborhood had departed in the last few years, desperately searching for those often disparaged "greener pastures." A better life. Any life in fact. Anything that could keep them housed with enough money left to actually graze those grassy dreams.

Silence—
she must have gone to get the paper.

Daisy pulled on her faded yellow dress—an old favorite—readying herself to set about the morning routine. Mundane hours of endless chores that would never be completed quite to satisfaction.

She leaned by the window, watching the slightly overweight, middle-aged man from next door sprint across the road. Always flirting with being late for work, always the last to go—except for Jimmy, her husband of nearly nineteen months. They'd been living here, with his mother since before they were married. An unpleasant, but unavoidable arrangement that began when the rent on Daisy's studio skyrocketed past Mars.

A lone bird remained. Late to breakfast, meekly scrounging for leftovers in piddling rain on the scrubby, square patch of matted grass that claimed to be the backyard. Blue iridescence. Strewn feathers glowed and glimmered mesmerizingly, accentuated by the overcast dimness of early morning.

Do birds think they are free?

If only she had a bit more faith in something. Politics, Jimmy, the weather. But everything seemed to be so pointless. Nothing changed for them, no matter how hard they tried.

The voices grew louder again. She paused in front of the kitchen door, plucking the courage to go in. As soon as her foot over the threshold, mother began on her daily routine.

"You're up late. I would think the least you could offer the poor old woman whose house you live in is a hot breakfast. I hear there might be a cashier job opening up at the supermarket. You should get yourself down there and tell the manager you want it. I know Mr. Saksby well. He can come down hard, and he expects you to work, but I'm sure if you put your mind to it..."

"You know very well I already have a job," Daisy replied curtly.

"That advertising, social mumbo jumbo whatever you call it? That's not a real job. You kids expect to get paid to play with your phone all day. Eleven hours on, six off, seven to sleep. Three breaks. That's work. Oh, that's nice. I see the laundry wasn't finished yesterday either.

My gran used to get it done in one day, and that was ironing and all. Never a wrinkle in one of daddy's shirts, or in one pillowcase."

"Mother," Jimmy muttered as he stood to leave for work, pushing the chair in quickly enough to produce a sharp, eardrum splitting screech.

Daisy walked him to the door as she did every day. He stopped suddenly, putting his hands on her shoulders and looking at her in such a deliberate way, she instinctively took a step back.

"Get our bags packed Daisy, we leave tomorrow night."
"Leave where? What do you mean?"
"The city. A real one. Chicago. New York. Wherever you want to go. You've put up with this long enough. I've finally saved up what we need to get out of here. Someplace better. Our own at least."

"I used to dream and I used to vow, I wouldn't dream of it now" — Morrissey, Glamorous Glue

"END"

Dr. Phil Asks About a High School Ex-Boyfriend
By Katie Darby Mullins

"When you base your whole identity/ on a reaction against somebody/ it's the same as being
in..."
-Sean Nelson, "The Same As Being In Love"

I haven't thought about him in so long, I don't know
how to start this poem: is the vague memory of ink stains
and the smell of cinnamon is enough to build a character
I don't fully remember? But then, every once in a while,
I'll get a burst of a moment, loud like a headache, lit up
in clear day: today I remember his car, maybe a Nissan?
Then it's gone.

       He's overseas now, and I had something
to do with that: a story I pretend to be proud of,
use to bolster my own ego, pretend I am strong. A catalyst.
But really, it was fear: of course it was fear. We don't
get rid of the people we can walk away from with no ties.
And I can't figure out why, now, Dr. Phil wants to know—
"Who is this boy in the picture?"
               "We all have albums full
of boys we don't talk to anymore," I say, waving him
away. The garage is crowded but the pictures are safe,
waterproof boxes. I try not to get lost out here, disappearing
into prom dress taffeta and vague forgotten faces.

Phil smiles and says, "These people make us who we are,"
and I cringe, because all I remember now is the ending:
Even that feels like a lie, somehow.
"It's like a hot stove," I say. "Not so close."
But then I remember the feeling of trouble-- knowing
that loving someone else was the worst risk I could ever take.
That even knowing someone loved me was dangerous.

And then that one moment,
when I told him I hated the rain, and he reached for me and pulled
me out into it, and danced with me in the mist. His leaning in
close, telling me my eyes were Elysian Fields, and even though
I smiled, all I could think of was how much I hated my clothes
growing ever damper against his chest, how much I couldn't wait
to let my thick hair down and loose in the car heater to dry.
How I made a quiet promise to myself never to tell him how much
I had to pretend so that he would like me. A promise that if, God

forbid, he ever left, that I would not compromise like that, never again.

The Poem Where Dr. Phil is in Reruns
By Katie Darby Mullins

Summer's lonely: the heat radiating off asphalt,
reflecting back at me when I look at my flip-flops.
I'm so much more used to staring at the TV
when I need to get out of my own mind, but even I
can't convince myself that I haven't seen today's argument
already—you know the one. The ex and his new woman,
stage left from his first wife, while they scream
about who screwed up their kids. (Kids who,
of course, are in the front row, faces tensed in pain.)
I must admit: I have probably seen this show twice,
but the fight, over and over, constantly, hundreds
of times, the same words, different faces, aging
in their bitterness. I try to conjure Phil, but he's gone—
vacationing somewhere I can't afford, even in dreams.

I'd like to ask him, though: why this story?
When your marriage has gone so well? Robin
sitting in the front row every day, polished and prim,
hair curled perfectly and never the same dress—
why do you bring so many broken people
to talk to each other this way in front of the world?
But I know why.
                    We don't always come by our
obsessions honestly. Sometimes they are handed
to us, like some horrible torch. My dog pulls
at the leash, reminding me that the sidewalk
is hot, and she'd rather spend her time running
than standing still. I wish I could say I was the same

The Angled Room
By Lee Smart

Pauline guided the rental van down the narrow country road. Hedges flanked it on either side and trees loomed over, blocking out the fading sunlight. The isolated road hadn't seen any traffic for a very long time; a thick deadfall of leaves carpeted the ill-maintained tarmac. Pauline slowed her speed as the van's tires slid and bounced over the potholed road. A soft moan came from the back of the van, barely muffled by the dividing plastic barrier behind her seat. Pauline cast her eyes back guiltily, listening for any more noise before focusing on the way ahead again.

How had she gotten to this point? It was the actions of one person, a monstrous act that sent her world spinning from its axis to crash down around her. Just one moment, and from it, everything she knew had shattered, unable to be fixed ever again. She couldn't change that, but there was one last chance she could grasp; one last way to reach out.

'Am I any better?' Pauline thought. *'I've not gone as far, but what I've done is nearly as bad. But I needed to do those things. And after it's all done, I'll do my best to put everything right. I won't hide or try to avoid what will come. I'll pay the price. I just need a little bit longer.'*

Even this close to her goal, uncertainty warred within her. She'd pinned all her hopes on nothing more than stories. Pauline had done things she'd never have considered doing before; taken actions that sickened her with disgust. But every time self-loathing rose up in her, it was met by the manic force of desperation in her heart. While these conflicting states spun inside her, she pushed forwards, intent on her destination. *'This is all I have now; I can't just walk away from it all.'* There would be consequences, and the police would be involved. She had made her peace with that outcome, and a sense of calm fatalism had fallen over her.

As long as she could do this last thing undisturbed, she would give herself up. *'Nothing else matters after tonight,'* she told herself. *'Either way, I'll know for sure. I have to try.'*

The trees began to thin as the road curved gently, revealing the peaked gable rooftops and tarnished metal finials of an old country mansion. The way ahead was barred by an iron gate, blooms of flaking red rust clinging to the metal. Drawing to a halt, Pauline switched off the engine and moved towards the gate on foot. The local flora had grown widely out of control; weeds and creepers had grown over the tall brick columns flanking the gate and along the iron fences to either side. Those fences, topped with spikes and too high to climb, disappeared into the thickening tree line on either side of the road. Pauline had done enough research to know the gate was the only way to reach the mansion.

Her eyes drawn to the corroded hinges, she carefully approached the gate and gave it an experimental push, but the metal held fast. Her heart raced at the thought she had come this far and would be denied, that everything she had done would be for naught. Fuelled by panic and frustration, she pushed harder against the gate. A long, drawn out creak was her reward as it swung open slightly, wobbling on its mountings. Pauline dug her heels into the ground and put all her weight into a shove. The gate moved another few inches and she repeated the process, finally creating a wide enough gap for the van with a last, torturous shriek from the hinges. Climbing back into the van, she turned the engine over and cautiously navigated through the gate.

The rough, unpaved road made the vehicle jump as Pauline drove up to the country house, her destination coming into full view before her. The mansion sat in a rough clearing, the road meandering towards a patch of gravel overgrown with weeds before it. She knew the house had been abandoned for more than a hundred years; no one had officially occupied it since then. What had been a palatial country estate on private land had become a foreboding, decrepit ruin reclaimed by nature and the elements. Manicured lawns and topiaries had grown out of control, and the plants of the surrounding forest had crept in to join them in colonising the exterior of the building. The house itself stood mostly intact; a testament to the skill of the builders and the strength of its stone. On the far side of the building, part of the roof had collapsed inwards, rotten beams showing like exposed bone around the damaged walls. Most of the windows still held glass, although they were encrusted with grime and filth. All of them were dark, no light or life showing within.

Pauline would normally have been surprised to find such a place abandoned. Its structure was sound and someone with money could have turned it into an opulent home once again. It was tucked away in a picturesque forest, but not so far from the local villages to render it remote. Just as surprising was the lack of any kind of damage from vandals. Aside from the effects of time and neglect, the mansion stood strong, almost as if it patiently awaited new occupants. There was something in the stone though, a disquieting sensation that lurked under the shadowed eaves and from the vacant windows that made her shudder. It was the reason why no one had tried to enter the mansion over the long years—that and the stories of what had happened there.

'If this was in the city,' she thought to herself, *'It would have been trashed. Graffiti, smashed windows, broken bottles, and used needles. The only damage here is from neglect. It'd be the perfect place to bed down if you were homeless, but something kept away vagrants too. This has to be the house; all the stories and urban legends are why people avoided coming here.'*

As far as Pauline knew, the derelict mansion was a shunned house.

Reaching a set of broad stone steps that led up the main doors, Pauline stopped the van. Taking a deep breath she closed her eyes and tried to calm down. If she were caught now she would be arrested, and probably jailed. She had been careful though; no one knew where she was or what she was doing. The house was miles from anywhere, the approaching dusk quiet and still. *'No one's coming to stop me—at least, not in time,'* Pauline thought. *'All I need is a little while longer and everything will be over. Not long now.'*

A gentle thump and a low groan from the back of the van spurred Pauline into action. She left the vehicle and moved towards the house. Walking up the first few steps, Pauline was struck by how quiet the area was: no birds sung, and even the usually buzzing insects were quiet. The house and the clearing it sat in were entirely silent save for the echo of her footsteps. The only movement apart from herself was that of the leaves and brush in the slight breeze. Pauline could have been standing in a photograph; the place felt like it had been frozen in a single moment, locked in stasis. An unquiet sensation bristled at the back of her mind and she swallowed, her throat suddenly dry. She wavered for a moment, her will ebbing before she steeled herself.
'Just this one thing,' she thought. *'Just one more little thing.'*
Pauline looked back at the van, pressed the button on the key fob again to make sure it was securely locked, and walked into the house.

An oppressive silence greeted her as she entered, as if the house itself were pressing down on her like a physical force. A dull reception hall spread out before her, the fading daylight barely illuminating the huge space. Wallpaper peeled in long, yellowing strips and a thick layer of dust coated every surface. Mould had begun to fur the worn rug in the centre of the hall and the air, full of drifting spores, had a dank, musty smell. Pauline stepped tentatively forward, her footsteps kicking up small clouds of dust.

"Hello?" she called out. "Is there anyone here?"

She hadn't expected to find any legal occupants in the mansion, but that didn't mean the house was empty. Such a large building could be a magnet for vagrants looking for somewhere dry to sleep or local youths exploring and drinking. That's if they were brave enough or hadn't heard the stories about the mansion. No one answered her; there were no sounds of creaking floorboards or opening doors. Pauline held her breath momentarily, listening to the silence around her. Nothing stirred in the ruined house and she breathed out again, satisfied she was alone. Taking a small torch from her pocket and flicking it on, she moved further into the cavernous hall. She played the beam of light across the room, dust motes floating through the stale air.

Old oil paintings, faded with age, still hung from the walls. Small ornaments, keepsakes from a previous occupant, cluttered wooden cabinets and sideboards. *'They really did leave in a hurry; it looks like everything they owned was abandoned here. Just what you'd expect from a haunted house.'* Pauline's research had revealed that the previous inhabitants had abandoned the house in one night. Something had happened there that had driven them out in a frantic rush, heedless of what possessions remained within its walls.

The light from her torch revealed a grand staircase at the back of the room. Thick balusters framed the wide stairs and a threadbare carpet, its colours washed to muted tones by time. The staircase diverged into two smaller ones at a narrow landing; the withered portrait of a dead patriarch hung on the wall between them. Pauline followed the staircase on the left, the echoes of her footsteps resounding from the walls. She reached a long, narrow hallway lined with doors and cast her torchlight down it. The shadows of plinth mounted busts and ornate picture frames skittered across the walls. A soiled curtain at the far end of the hall wafted in the breeze from a broken windowpane as she watched.

She felt her nerves begin to fray again, the seething emotions inside her desperate for her to run from the house. Loss, despair, fear and the rippling edge of mania warred within her. As she stared blankly down the empty hall, guilt crept back into her heart. *'What am I doing here? Chasing rumours and stories just because I can't let go?'* Had trauma really driven her so far? She might be losing her mind, but she couldn't let this chance go. If any of the stories about the house were true, she had to at least try. Afterwards, she would face the consequences her actions had earned. All she needed was a little more time. Pauline turned her focus from the hallway to a sheaf of papers she had pulled from her pocket. Unfolding it with shaking fingers, she peered at the words scrawled in her own spidery handwriting. Once she had memorized the instructions, Pauline carefully put them away again. Turning the torchlight back down the hall, she followed its beam down into the gloomy interior of the mansion.

Pauline passed through empty reception rooms filled with decaying furniture, water damaged, low couches and rotten oak tables filling the once opulent spaces. Her journey took her through the house library, an expansive two storey room filled with towering, dark oak bookcases. Hundreds of tomes populated its walls, many fallen to dust and decay over the decades. A few looked relatively intact, and she ran her fingertips across them. The leather-bound spines were soft with moisture and left a clammy, unclean feeling on her skin.

She continued on, stepping around toppled bookcases, their bases riddled with the small holes of woodworm.

Unease began to creep into her mind again. She was a fan of the supernatural, both fiction and supposedly true yarns. The mansion felt every inch a real life haunted house. From the lonely location to the dishevelled state of the interiors, it could have been lifted straight from one of her favourite novels. Pauline had always wanted to see a ghost, to touch the spirit world, but now she wasn't so sure. Being in this place, with the wind whistling through broken windows and empty halls, made her anxious. It brought to mind tales of vengeful wraiths and dark spirits.

"It's just nerves, that's all," she said aloud. "Anyone would be nervous in a place like this."

Even as she tried to control her fear, to keep the panic at bay, it scrabbled at the back of her mind as she walked the shadowed corridors. She drew a trembling hand across her forehead, beads of cold sweat slick under her palm, and walked further into the house.

After moving through several more rooms, Pauline finally found what she had been looking for. In the far wall of a wide parlour, its heavy curtains rotted through to let the last of the day's light in, was a large oak door. Most of the room's furniture had been piled against it, stacked hurriedly atop each other to keep the door from opening out into the room. Pauline knew the oak door was the only way in or out of the room beyond and, from the thick dust covering the makeshift barricade, no one had entered the space in years. She stared at the heavy door, it's oak panelled darkened and pitted with age, and a sudden surge of fear made her pause.

Someone had tried to keep something in that room, and even though anything in there would be long dead by now, Pauline still felt a wave of apprehension about going inside. Stepping warily towards the makeshift barricade, she ran her torch over the furniture, looking for a way to safely dismantle it. Pauline pulled on the leg of a heavy chair, the movement sending a shudder through the pile. She grasped the chair in both hands and pulled again, dragging it from the stack. Furniture crashed heavily to the floor and Pauline involuntarily jumped back as an avalanche of rotten wood snapped and splintered. The pile had scattered, leaving only a small cupboard against the door. Pauline moved through the wreckage, nudging pieces of jagged wood away with her feet then pushed the cupboard aside to reveal the entirety of the door.

It was heavy oak, stained dark with age, and as her torchlight flowed across it, she saw a shape was carved deeply into its upper half. A series of long straight lines had been cut precisely in the wood, each intersecting another so that a hollow shape was formed in their centre. It looked almost like a tunnel to Pauline's eyes, the angles of the lines and their size creating a false effect of receding from her. The cuts had been rendered in such a way that they seemed to move when she didn't look directly at them, giving her the sensation of slowly falling into the carved vortex.

"This is the room; it really did happen here," Pauline murmured.

Someone had taken a crude tool to the shape and severed some of the lines, bisecting them and ruining their angular beauty. This was what she had been searching for—if the stories were true. 'A way through, a way to communicate. That's all I need, just for a little while.' She reached out to touch the carving, pausing before her fingertips brushed it. The air between her fingers and the wood seemed to be gently vibrating, as if the lines were moving at impossible speed in the smallest of spaces. Pauline drew back, clasping her hand against her heart. She had to do this now; she'd come too far and done too much not to finish things. The stories of Fairholme House had drawn her in since she had first read them, and she had seized them like a lifeline. Now she would find out if they really were true.

'Just keep going,' she told herself. *'A few more steps, and this will all be over with. Anything after that doesn't matter now.'*

Pauline turned and walked back the way she had come, threading quietly through the rooms, until she reached the reception hall and the last part of what she planned to do in Fairholme House.

Dusk had fallen by the time Pauline reached the rental van. Her breath misted in the cool air as she took her backpack from the passenger seat. Pauline closed the door gently, leant on the side of the van, and took a deep breath to steady herself. The cool metal pressed into her forehead, and she slowly tried to gather her courage. Sickness grew in her stomach; a bitter taste that began to climb up her throat. Her face flushed with heat as a wave of disgust and nausea swept through her. She pounded her fist against the metal body of the van and a low whimper from inside brought her back to the moment. There was no going back now; just a little further and she'd get what she came here for.

'I've come too far to turn back now. I can do this for Teresa,' she thought as she clenched her fists white.

Stepping around to the back of the van, she flung the doors wide open to the night air. A terrified whimper drifted from the dark interior as Pauline took the torch from her pocket. The beam flickered briefly before steadying and illuminating the space inside. At the very back of the interior, as far from the doors as it was possible to get, was a young woman. Her ankles and wrists had been bound in thick tape, a strip plastered over her mouth as a gag to keep her from calling out. Her eyes were wide with terror, tear-stained makeup running down her face as she shuffled backwards away from Pauline. She mumbled something under her gag as Pauline stepped up into the vehicle and unsteadily moved towards the bound woman.

"Lydia, I'm sorry; I..." Pauline began as she stood over her.

Words deserted her as she looked down at the petrified woman. She looked into Lydia's eyes and saw she was deathly afraid of Pauline; a pure, deep, animal fear. No one had ever looked at her like that before, like she was an inhuman monster. Pauline didn't feel that she was in her heart; she'd just taken extreme measures for something so important to her it was worth the risk. She knew others might view her differently.

Lydia had worked at the supermarket with her for only a few months, not long enough for Pauline to form an attachment with the young woman. It was the main reason Pauline chosen her: she'd hoped a lack of emotional involvement would make things easier. That and the fact that despite being nearly twenty, Lydia was short and slim. It would be easier for Pauline to carry her into the house.

As she crouched next to Lydia, Pauline took a small plastic bag from her coat pocket, its contents a clear, thick liquid. The girl struggled frantically against her bonds, the muffled cries from under her gag rising in pitch. Awkwardly grabbing the back of Lydia's head, Pauline opened the bag and held it against the girl's nose until her eyes closed and her struggles ceased.

Pauline held the bag there a moment longer, then removed it and leaned in, carefully listening to Lydia's regular soft breaths.

Grateful Lydia was still alive and that she hadn't used too much chloroform, Pauline pocketed the bag once again. She knew little about how much of the chemical to use, only that it was a makeshift tranquilliser based on what she had seen in the movies. Getting it had been easier than she thought, but she was still terrified of using too much and accidentally killing Lydia. Pauline threaded her arms under the unconscious girl's shoulders and legs, lifting her with surprising ease. Lydia weighed next to nothing; although she was an adult, she had the build and height of a young teenager. Pauline carefully stepped from the van with her burden, a momentary slip of her foot on the leaf strewn ground sending her tumbling forward.

She managed to keep hold of Lydia, but ended up on her knees with the woman resting across them. Her gaze lingered on Lydia's face, strands of dark hair plastered across it, the skin around her cheeks and chin pinched by the tape gag. Her skin pale in the fading light, Lydia looked peaceful. *'Peaceful and innocent,'* Pauline thought. A flutter moved through her chest. Had Teresa looked like this, innocent and scared, at the end? What the hell was she doing, kidnapping an innocent girl, someone barely older than her sister? Guilt rose up in her with the taste of bile, and her emotions raged. Anger, loss, and self-loathing collided inside her heart. Could she really do this, go through with it all?

The memory of a morning months past, of a phone call and the collapse of her world, pierced her doubt like a spear. Pauline took a deep breath, weighed what she was about to do against what she had lost and could bring back, and made her choice. Lydia didn't deserve this, but neither did Teresa deserve the fate she had gotten. And Teresa was her sister. *'I don't really have a choice,'* Pauline thought to herself. Her train of thought absolved her feelings of guilt again, and she stood, cradling Lydia tight to her body. Pauline angled the young woman nearer to her, gently resting Lydia's head on her shoulder, and walked up the stairs into the mansion.

The darkened rooms and corridors of Fairholme house welcomed Pauline back with their restive silence. She moved as quickly as she could, carrying Lydia through the building and back to the room with the carved door. Gently laying her unconscious charge on a dusty chaise-lounge, Pauline took the torch from her pocket and approached the door. She pushed against it, the subtle vibration she had felt earlier travelling up her arm like the tickle of insectile legs. The door gave slowly; rusted hinges squealed as a shadowed space was revealed beyond. It was an abysmal darkness, thick and cloying, its depths seeming to resist the illumination of her torch.

The room behind the door was small compared to the rest of the house, barely twenty feet square. A toppled wooden chair sat to one side, grime and dust covering its delicate frame. Pauline stepped inside, turning a slow circle and casting the thin torch beam over the interior. It was bare apart from the chair, the thick red carpet worn and moth-eaten with age. It crackled under Pauline's footsteps like desiccated skin, the noise loud in the tomb-like silence of the room. The walls were lined in the same dark wood she'd seen in the rest of the mansion, and free of any kind ornamentation.

Except for the lines.

Across the walls were a riot of lines, intersecting and crossing each other in some complex design. They had been carved an inch deep into the wall, deep trenches sunk into the wood panelling. Pauline pressed a fingertip into the nearest one; it was easily wide enough to admit her finger and was cut down to the brick work beneath. The same slight vibration was there, like a soft gust of air whistling through a crack in a window. It flowed in one direction, threading down the cut towards the far side of the room from the door. Pauline pulled her fingertip from the line, angling the torchlight along the wall instead. As she turned in place, she saw other lines converged with it until they joined in a single shape on the wall opposite the door.

It was a similar design to the one on the door to the room, but vastly more intricate. Hundreds of straight lines crossed each other to create a whirlpool-like shape in the wooden panels. The lines were angled in such a way that they created the impression of a vortex receding away from the centre of the room. It seemed as if the rear wall led into a geometric cave of angled lines that sought to draw in anyone who looked upon them. Pauline felt a moment of vertigo, as though she were standing at the edge of a great precipice and about to fall forward. The vortex danced in her peripheral vision, the angled lines seeming to move glacially slowly when she wasn't looking directly at them. For a moment, Pauline had the impression the room was contracting around her like a gigantic throat. Her balance disappeared and she fell, landing hard on her rump.

Pauline fought the urge to vomit, clamping her jaw tightly closed, and staggered to her feet. That was when she saw part of the carved vortex had been damaged. Several lines near its centre had been disrupted, the wooden panels splintered by the repeated strikes of some heavy tool. The perfect, nauseating geometry of the vortex had been ruined, the vandalism somehow robbing it of its full power. Pauline's balance returned as she looked at the broken sections and she moved closer to them to inspect the damage. She was so intent on the angled design that she nearly fell again when her foot struck a heavy object on the floor. Looking down, she saw a short hatchet covered in cobwebs, the blade pitted and rusted.

Pauline picked it up, turning it over in the torchlight. A thought crossed her mind and she placed the blade of the hatchet into the brutally marked wood of the wall. It fit perfectly, its smile disappearing into the wood. The axe had obviously been used to disrupt the design, and done so in a frenzy, judging by the splintered wood. Pauline cast the hatchet aside, the dull thump of its landing echoing from the walls. *'This is the place,'* she thought to herself. *'This is the angled room from the stories.'*

"Teresa, I hope you can hear me," she said softly.

Pauline emptied her bag, placing a portable electric lantern in the centre of the room and lighting the space in a yellow glow. She placed her tools on the floor by the vortex and left the room to collect Lydia. The girl was still unconscious, her eyes moving rapidly under their lids as though she was dreaming. Pauline carried her into the angled room, carefully resting her in a sitting position in a corner opposite the vortex. Lydia slumped against the wall, her head resting next to one of the carved lines.

Pauline moved back to the vortex and took up her tools. She'd brought a large, thick chisel and mallet, both heavy but perfectly suited to the task ahead. Pauline rested the head of the chisel against the first damaged section of the vortex and struck it with the mallet. The cracking of wood rang out as Pauline hammered over and over again. She repaired the damage, chipping away the panelling and cutting the line deep into the bricks beneath. The vortex had been broken in several places and Pauline chiselled at the wall relentlessly, completing the pattern with her furious effort.

It was full dark by the time Pauline had repaired all of the lines bar one. She was sweating heavily from the exertion, and her breath sawed out through clenched teeth. Something in the air had changed every time she'd repaired one of the lines, the far off whistling they carried seeming to draw closer. It still sat just below a whisper, like a hunting cry carried on the wind, ready to break out into a rising shriek. Pauline dropped the tools from her tired hands and turned to where she had left Lydia. The corner was empty. At some point, Lydia had awoke and carefully crawled across the room, most of her body now out of the door. Pauline dashed towards her, grasping the girl's ankles tightly. Lydia twisted round, her eyes wide with terror as Pauline tried to drag her back. The bound woman thrust her hands in the pile of twisted furniture beyond the door, frantically trying to escape.

Pauline's compassion for her co-worker evaporated, replaced with anger and desperation. She'd come too far now to go back; she needed Lydia and couldn't let her get away. Jerking her captive's legs back, she pulled the woman into the angled room, grunting with the effort. Pauline looked up in time to see Lydia drag her hands from the wrecked furniture, a short chair leg clutched between them. Lydia's wide blow sailed down towards Pauline's head, and she tumbled sideways, the improvised cudgel striking a glancing blow on her scalp.

The world darkened and shook for a moment as Pauline staggered to the floor. She was dimly aware of Lydia shuffling away on all fours and put a hand to her head, her palm bloodied by the shallow cut on her scalp. Pauline shook her head, clearing her vision, and lunged after Lydia. Anger boiled in her and she knocked the girl's chair leg weapon away, straddling her and punching her viciously across the jaw. Pauline threw another punch, driven by the emotional turmoil raging in her, and Lydia collapsed to the floor, one nostril blooded and swollen. The young woman looked at her with pure terror, blood and tears running down her face.

Pauline froze, shocked at what she had done. She had never been a violent person; she'd never even thrown a punch before. Where had this anger come from? This rage? It had been borne of desperation, of an all-consuming need for something. Pauline stood, weeping in shame and reached a trembling hand out to Lydia. The girl flinched and whimpered, terrified beyond measure. A wave of disgust swamped Pauline and she began to babble.

"I'm sorry; so, so sorry," she mumbled. "I... I... didn't mean to."

Lydia tried in vain to move away, to escape, but necessity overtook Pauline and she dragged the bound girl back into the room. She ignored the dull thumps of Lydia's head bouncing from the door frame and left her in the centre of the room. The girl rolled on the floor, moaning gently under her gag, her wordless pleading followed Pauline as she strode over and closed the door. She rejoined Lydia, kneeling between the girl and the carved vortex. Lydia had stilled, looking at Pauline before her gaze moved over the chisel and mallet, and the hatchet in the corner. The girl began to weep more freely, the tape of the gag twisting and distorting as she tried to speak. Pauline looked at her discarded tools and realised the young woman was begging for her life. Her actions were terrifying to her co-worker; the work of a deranged predator with sick appetites. Pauline leant forward and brushed some of Lydia's sweat-dampened hair from her face.

"I'm not going to hurt you; I promise," Pauline said tremulously.

Lydia didn't seem to believe her. The young woman stayed still, not attempting to move away, but still breathing in strained snorts over her gag.

"I need your help." Pauline continued. "It's important. I couldn't just ask someone to help me. What I need... it's too much to ask. That's why I had to bring you here. You'll be safe though. I just have to do something and then you can go. You can call the police, get away from here. I won't deny what I've done. I just need a little longer, that's all."

Lydia rolled onto her side and tried again to speak through her gag. Although the girl was still scared, it sounded to Pauline like she was asking a question.

"Why did I do this?" Pauline asked. "It's... it's complicated. I'll sound mad, but I'm really not. I bet you think I am, right?"

Pauline laughed, a reedy and shrill sound, hysteria worrying at its edges. Lydia was shaking her head wildly. Pauline knew her co-worker thought she was insane by now and was just agreeing to do what she could to save herself from harm. Pauline took a deep breath that caught in her throat and broke into tears.

"I have—I had... a sister," she began.

"Her name was Teresa, and she was a little younger than you. She was smart and beautiful, just a lovely person. She'd do anything for anyone. Teresa was studying at university last year; she wanted to be an engineer. We were so proud of her. The first one in our family to go to uni. I was proud of her too; she was going to do something with her life, go places and see things. Not like me. Teresa and I were really close; even though she was younger, she was the confident one. I always wanted to be more like her.'"

Pauline's voice had dropped to a whisper, the sound loud in the still air of the room. Lydia had stopped shuffling on the floor, her attention fully on her captor, eyes wide and wary.

"One morning, eight months ago, I got a phone call from my mum. She was in tears, hysterical..." Pauline continued, weeping freely now.

"The police had contacted her; they'd found a body—Teresa's body. Some kids had found her in a back alley, half buried under bin bags. Teresa had been strangled. The police think it had been a robbery or attempted assault, she'd fought back, and her attacker had killed her. Just like that. This beautiful person, a light on the world, just snuffed out. Everything she could've been ended instantly. The police never found who did it, but even that wouldn't have helped."

Wiping her tears with the sleeve of her coat, Pauline took several steadying breaths before carrying on.

"My world just stopped. I couldn't... I couldn't go on. I just kept thinking about Teresa's last few moments. Scared, alone... dying. If I was there, maybe I could've protected her. I wasn't though; I wasn't there for her. Losing someone like that, you just can't get over it. That loss changes you, like a shattered mirror it leaves you crooked and in pieces. You can't be put back together. I had a breakdown, had counselling, and got prescribed drugs. No matter what I tried, I couldn't let Teresa go. When it got really bad, I thought about killing myself to be with her again. You see, I've never had a lot of friends; I don't have a boyfriend or anything. Teresa was my link to the world, to other people. Without her I'm just... alone."

Pauline pulled her knees to her chest, folding her arms tightly around herself.

"I didn't have the strength for suicide—I'm just too weak. I started speaking to Teresa as if she was still here; I thought maybe, wherever she was now, she might hear me. I just wanted to speak to her again. That was the start of this journey. I went to a few of those psychic stage shows, and the mediums who say they can talk to the dead. But no message ever came through for me. I even tried Ouija boards and séances; all the things I'd dismissed as nonsense before Teresa was murdered. I just wanted one more chance to speak to her again."

Pauline looked up at Lydia, the girl lit starkly by the lamp. She was lying on her left side, a thin line of blood running from one nostril. The girl was too scared to move or attempt another escape. She looked at Pauline as if she'd truly lost her mind, that any action on Lydia's part might trigger another beating or worse. Pauline stifled a sob and answered her captive's unspoken judgment.

"I'm not mad, Lydia. I just miss Teresa so much. I know I should let her go and move on, but that felt too much like forgetting her. I... I couldn't do that. So I kept looking, until I finally found something.

"Welcome to Fairholme Park House," Pauline said, gesturing to the room with her hands. "Built in 1820 as the country retreat for Edward Marcus Fairholme, an industrialist who made his fortune in iron. After it was completed, he spent a great deal of time here with his wife, Jessica, before she passed away in an accident. She fell down the grand staircase, and broke her neck. Fairholme just couldn't take her loss... like me and Teresa, I guess. He had a lot more money than me, and was obsessed with speaking to his wife again."

Pauline kept a close eye on Lydia as she spoke. The girl had ceased to struggle but was glancing around the room when she thought Pauline wasn't looking. Whether for a way out or another improvised weapon, Pauline didn't know, but she couldn't let her leave now, she was too close.

"The story goes that many months after her death, she appeared to him in his dreams. She tried to speak to him, to tell him something. These dreams got stronger and stronger, until finally her message got through. Jessica told him of a way they could talk again, past the barrier of death. It was so simple. She told him it was all down to the angles; that the universe was made of intersecting shards and angles and by drawing the right ones they could be together. It just required patience and the correct lines in the correct positions. All just to make the right shape to open the door from here to... *there*."

Turning, Pauline pointed at the angled vortex carved into the wooden wall behind her.

"That shape."

Lydia frowned in confusion as Pauline stood and walked to the vortex. She caressed the lines cautiously, feeling the pull of air run through each roughly hewn trench in the wood.

"Fairholme kept copious notes on his research, all the little details of his plan. I found people online who had copies, although they believed it was all urban legends and tall stories. They didn't have what I had, that motivation. A sense of hope, a truly desperate need. All I knew was I had a chance. Even if it was all horseshit, I had to try. If it was true, it meant I could talk to Teresa again. So I kept digging. I found a few scattered pages of Fairholme's diary in an online archive, nothing of interest to anyone unless they knew what they were looking for. It detailed his attempts here, his methods, what he managed to do. Fairholme wrote that he had succeeded, he had spoken to Jessica, and the diary entries were filled with his hope to communicate more."

Pauline began to trace to the carved lines with her fingertips, lost in her own story.

"After Fairholme's first few attempts, the diary entries stopped abruptly. I looked for any other information on this place; any clue as to what might have happened. There was an article in a local newspaper; it mentioned an incident at the house but not in great detail. Three servants died and Fairholme left for his house in the city, never to return here again. Over the years, stories were told about the house: there were noises at night, ghostly figures seen wandering the halls. Every so often, a curious local or explorer would witness something inexplicable. It was because of what had happened here: Fairholme had reached the other side and the way through was still open. He had managed to talk to someone he had lost, someone who'd died. That was all I needed to know."

Dropping her hands to her sides, Pauline exhaled loudly, trying to calm her highly-strung nerves and racing thoughts.

"This is the room it happened in, the angled room from Fairholme's diary. He carved the lines into the wall himself; all of them culled from the dreams his wife sent him. They had to be precise, every angle exactly right to tunnel through to the beyond. Now we're here, I can feel it. This isn't a fake or some kind of scam; this is real. You can feel it, can't you? We're close to something that's normally far, far away from our everyday lives. Teresa's near to us and that vortex will open the way."

Lydia shrunk back as Pauline crossed the room and crouched down before her. She tried her best to sound calm, to not scare her co-worker any more than she had already. The girl just looked at her with undisguised fear, a glint in her eyes that was tinged with rising anger. '*It won't be long before she tries to get away again,*' Pauline thought wearily to herself. She had to hurry and finish what she had started before she ran out of time.

"I'm sorry I kidnapped you. I didn't want to hurt you and I promise as soon as we are done here, I'll let you go. Nothing bad is going to happen to you. I didn't mean to hit you. Things will be okay; you'll see," Pauline babbled at the bound woman. "I just need your help with one more thing."

Pauline reached for her backpack, fumbling inside for something.

"You see, Fairhome's diaries said the dead can't just talk; they need to speak through someone. They need a body, a voice. That's... that's why I need you. You have to be Teresa's voice here. I need your help, Lydia."

The dull metal of the utility knife glinted in the light as Pauline pulled it from her backpack. Lydia saw it and began to scream under her gag, the muffled noise like the cries of a drowning victim. Tendons and veins corded on the neck of the bound woman, each one full of life and ready to split under the edge of the knife. Lydia screamed and screamed, thrashing her arms and legs, banging her head on the floor, frantically pleading for her life with wordless, muted howls.

Pauline extended the blade from the body of the knife, the dry clack of the mechanism like a snapping bone. She advanced on Lydia, the knife held low in one shaking fist. Lydia pushed herself awkwardly away from Pauline, but resistance was hopeless. The tears in her eyes ran over her bloodied nose as her captor loomed above her, the knife raised high. Pauline watched as Lydia sobbed and shook, mouthing pleas for help, for her mother, for a few minutes more life under the tight embrace of the tape over her lips.

Pauline brought the utility knife down in a wide glittering arc.

Lydia screamed one last time; her eyes squeezed shut as she waited to feel the blade cut into her flesh. Instead, she heard a sharp, stifled cry and something warm spattered on her face. She opened her eyes and looked up at Pauline. The woman had sliced the knife across the palm of her other hand, the wound bleeding freely and bright red in the harsh white light. Pauline bit down on her lower lip and pocketed the utility knife. She ran her index finger through her own blood, taking a large smear of it from her palm.

Lydia sat stock still, disturbed by Pauline's act of self-mutilation. She felt small relief that she hadn't been cut and that Pauline had put the knife away but was still wary and terrified of her captor.

Pauline knelt down, taking Lydia's chin in her wounded hand and gripping her tightly. The girl winced as Pauline's nails dug into the soft skin of her face and warm blood painted her chin. Slowly and with great care, Pauline drew an elaborate geometric shape onto Lydia's forehead, the mirror of the carved vortex behind them. Lydia cried, stiffening against the disgust she felt at having a mad woman smear blood across her face. Finishing the design, Pauline released her prisoner and walked back to the carved wall. She picked up the chisel and mallet and stood at the centre of the vortex.

"I told you I wouldn't hurt you, Lydia. You'll speak for Teresa. There has to be some sacrifice, but it has to come from me. My blood links me to Teresa; it'll help her find us," Pauline said with a short bark of laughter.

"It's ridiculous, isn't it? I read a lot—ghost stories mostly. Blood sacrifices, summoning, spells… it seems some of it is right after all."

Lydia looked on, her face a mixture of confusion and fear, exhaustion creeping into her tortured gaze. Pauline turned back to the wall, resting the chisel over the final damaged line. She struck at it, driving the tool into the brickwork beneath the wood repeatedly. The whistling she had heard earlier increased, hovering just below the level of her hearing. It sounded far off, but barrelling closer like a charging animal.

Something was coming towards them.

As Pauline worked at the line, Lydia saw tiny violet sparks begin to dance within the lines around the room, the colour running to a cold blue and back again. The air thrummed like a struck chord and the pressure in the room thickened, its weight like the abysmal depths of the ocean. Pauline struck the chisel one last time, completing the design. She stepped back from the vortex, casting the tools aside. Shafts of neon violet and ice blue light shone through the angled lines, transfixing her. The whistling rose and quickly she remembered what she needed to do.

Scrabbling across the room, Pauline crashed to the floor next to Lydia and pulled the tape roughly from the co-worker's face. She gripped Lydia's shoulders tight as the girl struggled in her grasp.

"Please, just let me go. I won't tell anyone. I just want to go home, please... please..." Lydia mumbled weakly.

"Teresa!" Pauline called as she shook the girl. "Teresa! It's me, Pauline; your sister!"

Lydia wept, her body ragdoll limp as Pauline shook her in a frenzy, calling her dead sister's name. The whistling around them rose in pitch, the light illuminating them from every side, banishing the shadows. The girl suddenly stiffened, her eyes going slack and unfocussed, the bloody design on her forehead glowing with motes of purple light. Pauline froze, holding her breath expectantly.

"I can see them..." Lydia whispered hoarsely. "They're near now... coming nearer..."

"Teresa! Please, speak to me!" shouted Pauline. "I'm here; please, come back!"

"They want us... want to step inside... to wear. We are... we are meat to them," Lydia whispered.

Suddenly, the whistling rose to a painful crescendo and the light flared like a nuclear blast. Lydia's body went taut, as though an electric current raged through it, and her eyes rolled back to expose their whites. Pauline screamed as the electric lantern shorted out in a flurry of sparks and a torrent of wind spun through the room, carrying dust and dirt in a blistering tornado. The whistling hit a fever pitch and fragmented into competing sounds, a manic, idiot piping of shrill cries. As the violent light flooded the room, Pauline was flung from Lydia, thrown through the air, and bouncing hard into a wall. She shut her eyes against the light, but it shone through the thin skin of her eyelids until the whole world was a purple-white void.

Pauline screamed, long and loud, her voice matching the swirling, schizophrenic piping that invaded her ears. She felt something drop toward her, the air pressure becoming heavier and weighted. All the small, terrified, animal part of her brain would allow her to do was scream, and Pauline tasted blood as something in her throat tore. Everything around her raged: light, sound, and pressure building to a terrible peak. Pauline felt blood run freely from her nose and ears as she pushed her body into the deep carpet, trying in vain to escape the sensory assault around her.

Then the world shattered like a massive pane of glass being struck, and everything went dark.

It could've been minutes or hours later when Pauline surfaced back into awareness. She blinked rapidly, grogginess fading from her mind like a lazy tide. Struggling to stand, her head resonating with a sharp ringing, Pauline looked over the room. The whistling had stopped, and the light had faded to dull molten glow within the carved angles of the walls that barely illuminated the blackness. The only light came from the ruined electric lantern as it cast a fitful glow. It had been damaged and flashed like a strobe light, causing Pauline's movements to look jumpy and stuttered.

She saw a crumpled shape in the far corner of the room, the malfunctioning light enough for her to tell it was Lydia. Whether dead or unconscious, she didn't know and a sudden panic gripped her heart.

"Teresa?" she called softly. "Are you there? Teresa, it's Pauline. Answer me, please."

Pauline staggered towards Lydia, her steps slow and painful after being thrown across the room. She neared the woman and reached out to her when a high, girlish giggle stopped her in place. Pauline was sure it had come from Lydia; absolutely certain it had when the voice giggled again. It had the light airy tone of an amused child, but with something darker underneath.

"Teresa?" asked Pauline, her heart in her throat.

"*No, no,*" Lydia replied with a breathless laugh.

"Lydia?"

"*Not that one either. More than that.*"

Pauline stopped mid-step as Lydia rose. The girl had been lying on her right side, facing away from Pauline. Her head and shoulders angled up from the floor, like a puppet picked up by invisible strings. Lydia's legs drew up under her, crouching and propelling her to a standing position. Something about the motion was subtly wrong and Pauline took a step back. Lydia cocked her head to one side then the other, as though experimenting with the range of movement.

"Who are you?" Pauline asked.

"*No, no names. No others. Others but not apart from us... fragments of one,*" Lydia replied.

Then the kidnapped girl turned to face her and Pauline screamed until faintness threatened to claim her.

Something looked out at Pauline from behind Lydia's eyes, but it was not her young co-worker. The girl's eyes were black with sparks of violet light, the colours of the iris and sclera blanketed by a dark void. Lydia's small, narrow mouth had distended into a wide, feline smile. Her gums bloody where too many teeth like glass needles had pushed through them. As she approached, her features seemed to stutter like a time-lapse film.

"You're not Teresa," Pauline gasped. "I called for Teresa; where is she?!"

"*And you are not Ead-Ward-Feah-Alm,*" Lydia replied, seeming to struggle with pronouncing the name.

"What are you?!" Pauline asked, crying and on the verge of hysterics.

"*You called to us. Across the outside. You made the angles, made the gate... we came from our shards... out from the black pyramids under the Pentangle Star.*"

Lydia stepped closer to Pauline who remained rooted to the spot. The girl raised one pale hand to her own face and the fingers flickered, moving at an inhumanly fast speed.

"*You let us into... down from the deep dark. We ride in the Lid-ee-ahh; we have been away so very long... away in the angles... away from the warmth of your space... away from the... meat.*"

Pauline shook with fear, tears running down her face as Lydia's hand began to deform and stretch. The index finger became a long, crooked claw, the tip splitting into two curved nails.

"We need more... more meat... more for the others in our shard to ride into this space. More than Lid-ee-ahh..."

Pauline paced back from the thing that had been Lydia as it walked towards her. She was so focussed on the monstrosity that she lost her footing and tumbled to the floor. Lydia hunched, tensing her shoulders like an animal ready to pounce. She let out another high-pitched laugh and leapt at her prey. In the split second before the monster landed on her, Pauline flailed her arms across the carpet, her hand grasping the wooden handle of something. The finger claws of the Lydia were inches from Pauline's eyes when she swung her arm at her attacker. The rusted hatchet in her hand slammed into Lydia's shoulder with the sound of breaking mirrors.

Lydia stumbled back with a shrill cry, clutching her injured shoulder as Pauline pushed herself up off the floor. Pauline breathed heavily, the hatchet clutched tight against her chest as she backed away. The cries of the Lydia dissolved back into giggles and she turned to face Pauline. The hatchet wound on her shoulder hadn't bled; it had *splintered*. Where the small axe had parted flesh, it had become jagged shards of matter; small, angled shapes fell from it to break on the floor like glass. The angles and cracks spread over the girl's chest giving her the appearance of a living stained glass window. Each shape around the wound was subtly out of sync with the others. It was as if Lydia's body was made of many small windows into another world, and Pauline's attack had knocked the view askew.

Lydia examined at her shoulder, pawing at it with one long claw. She looked back at Pauline and laughed like a struck pane of glass.

"Not all us, not all you... harder to break... shatter, yes, but not break... more angles to bring more through..." she said.

Pauline screamed hysterically and flung the hatchet at the monster. It sailed past her former co-worker as the girl leapt again, embedding itself in the one of the lines at the edge of the carved vortex. The effect on the monster was instantaneous. Lydia stuttered in mid-air, her form a badly cut out image overlaid on reality. She screamed, a high, shrieking note, and fell to the ground. Pauline stepped back as Lydia shook spasmodically, looking from her palsied form to the hatchet buried in the wall. Its blade had partially severed one of the lines, cutting through half of its thick width.

'Lydia needs the vortex lines to be intact to stay here,' Pauline thought. *'She told me as much herself. I repaired the lines and let her in.'* Realisation hit Pauline. If she could destroy the angled lines in the wall, then maybe she could stop Lydia and send back whatever had taken her body. She moved past the juddering girl, careful to stay out of reach of her clawed hands. It looked as if Lydia's seizures were diminishing, as though the thing inside her was reasserting control. The monster locked a hate-filled stare on Pauline and let out a lowing, predatory bellow.

Pauline rushed to the wall, taking up the chisel and mallet and began to hammer away at the lines. Each time she severed one, crude strokes chopping into the wood, Lydia let out another pained yell of anger. Pauline had damaged several with her frantic hammering, her own breath loud in her ears, when she realised Lydia had stopped crying out. She had barely turned back when what felt like a whip of crystal teeth lashed at her shoulder blades. Pauline screamed and fell to the floor, the warm wetness of her own blood soaking into her shredded coat. She rolled to the side in time to avoid a follow up blow, dirt and wooden splinters digging into her wound.

Lydia stood over her, yelling incoherently as her body slipped and strobed in place. It was obvious to Pauline that whatever was inside Lydia was losing its grip on the girl and fighting like a cornered animal. The monster kept lashing out desperately and only its lack of co-ordination saved Pauline from further harm. As Lydia slashed a claw at her, Pauline rolled again, moving out of the way of the attack. She kicked out hard, connecting with Lydia's kneecap, the sound of crashing glass ringing out with the blow. Lydia toppled, already over-balanced from her previous strike, and smashed into the floor.

She scrambled to her feet as Lydia spasmed on the floor, the girl struggling to rise. Pauline struck her across the back of the head with the mallet and Lydia cried out again. Dropping the mallet, Pauline rushed to the door of the room. She barrelled through it, knocking aside the makeshift furniture barricade outside. Pauline lost her footing, pitching forward before she caught herself. Behind her, in the angled room lit fitfully by the damaged lantern, she saw Lydia stand drunkenly.

Pauline wasted no time and ran farther into the house, trying her best to find the way out from memory. She upended small pieces of furniture as she ran, dizzy from blood loss and pain. From somewhere behind her came the hunting shrieks of Lydia, each one sounding closer from the last. Pauline ran down another dark hallway, staggering at the end and rebounding from the wall as she tried to turn the corner on faltering legs. She left bloody handprints behind as she pushed off the wall, anxiously looking for anything familiar that might point the way outside. Pauline kept running through the abandoned house until a thin sliver of moonlight appeared up ahead.

Charging for the safety of the night outside, Pauline had almost reached the main door when a crooked form slammed into her. She was dragged to the floor in a razored grip, sharp edges cutting painfully into her arms. Pauline struck out at Lydia, her blows splintering the girl's glass-flesh. Lydia straddled Pauline, swiping maniacally with her clawed hands. She did her best to block the blows, but one angled finger cut a line along her collarbone. Pauline cried out as blood splashed over her in an arc. The girl looked down at Pauline, insanity dancing in her eyes as a wide grin split her face.

Lydia knocked Pauline's arms aside, fastening her hands around the pinned woman's throat. Pauline felt the sharp edges of Lydia's palms recede and soften. The girl didn't want her to die quickly from a cut throat, but slowly, choking for air in her monstrous grasp. Lydia nodded slowly with sadistic glee at the understanding she saw in Pauline eyes. The girl tightened her grip and Pauline felt something inside her throat begin to deform. Lydia tensed her arms, leaning her full weight down onto her former captor.

Pauline fumbled in her pockets as her vision started to grey at the edges. The pressure behind her eyes was immense and her mouth worked soundlessly, trying to draw in air. She felt a familiar shape in her pocket and grasped cold metal. Just as unconsciousness rose up like a black tide, she pulled her hand from her pocket and sent it slashing towards Lydia's neck. The small blade of the utility knife glittered in the moonlight before it cut into the left side of the girl's neck. Flesh parted and snapped, blood like small rubies falling from the severed artery.

The crystal drops of blood tumbled down Pauline's arm like hailstones and fell to shatter against the wooden floor. The vice grip around her neck slackened and she gulped in a great draught of air. Her vision returned, blurs of colour becoming more defined. Pauline's hand still held the knife, its cutting edge embedded deeply in Lydia's neck. The girl was unmoving, still sitting atop her but slack and doll-like. Lydia's eyes were vacant, her hands resting on Pauline chest and twitching slightly.

Warm liquid ran down Pauline's arm and she glanced at the ruby waterfall that was cascading from the girl's injury. The small gems were softening and becoming fluid again. Lydia's body shook once and the change spread out from her wound, the angled shards turning to human flesh once again. When the effect reached the hatchet wound on Lydia's shoulder, blood ran freely from it. The girl looked dumbly down and Pauline saw the malevolent, animating force inside her had fled. Whatever dark entity had taken Lydia's body was gone now, and the girl was dying. Lydia tried to speak; her lips parted but only a small, pained moan escaped them.

The girl fell from her position on Pauline, boneless like a puppet with cut strings. Pauline screamed and scrambled away, weeping as Lydia fell alongside her. She cast aside the bloody knife and crawled away from Lydia's body. The full horror and enormity of what she had done hit her. She had committed exactly the same act as Teresa's killer had. Pauline had taken a young woman's life as if it was nothing, because her own need was more important than another person. She had just wanted to speak to her sister again and never meant for it all to come to this.

This wasn't what she had wanted.

"I'm sorry... sorry... so sorry, Teresa," she whimpered pathetically to herself.

Her blood-covered hands slipped as she pulled herself up the doorframe and into a standing position. Pauline's mind, already tortured and frayed from losing her sister, fractured completely. She wailed, beating her fists against her head as the memory of Teresa, cold on a mortuary slab, melted into the bloody image of Lydia's body. Stumbling into the garden, she dropped to her knees, lightheaded and unable to process what she had done.

'This is too much, I didn't mean for this to happen,' she thought. *'I can't... it's too much...'* She wanted to blot it all out, to just go away from the world. The things she had done, the pain she'd caused, was too much to acknowledge. She'd killed Lydia; an innocent woman taken by something inhuman. The girl would still be alive right now if she'd just been able to let go of Teresa. She knew her lost sister would never forgive her for such a thing, and Lydia would have no chance to either. Pauline would never forgive herself. She was a murderer; no better than the monster that had killed Teresa. Pauline couldn't go on after what she had done; she wanted to die.

She searched the ground around her for the utility knife before remembering she'd left it somewhere in the house. Pauline fell forward; her face buried in the soft soil of the garden and let out a deep wail of despair. Hot tears mixed with the muddy ground and her chest was wracked with sobs. She lay there, overwhelmed with horror and disgust for hours. By the time sunlight began to dance through the trees, her mind had fallen blank, the acts she'd committed too much to cope with.

Pauline moved robotically towards her rented van, dimly aware of her surroundings and driven on by simple instinct. Her hand brushed the driver's door handle when a sound brought her back to the world. A scratching noise, like a fingernail on glass, echoed across the garden. She turned on the spot, seeking its source. It seemed to be all around her, growing more and more insistent. A slight movement drew her attention to the van's side window. Thin, sharp lines were appearing in the glass, carved by invisible talons. The lines appeared quicker, clustering around each other to form a twisting vortex on the window.

"The way is open now... for us... for all of us..." hissed a disembodied, sibilant voice.

Pauline screamed at the sensation of thousands of glass splinters passing through the meat of her mind. She shuddered, blood running from her eyes and ears. Her vision blurred, doubled, and fractured into a compound eye view of the world. Pauline felt a horrible sense of wrenching dislocation, of falling away from everything around her to somewhere deeper. Somewhere darker. Clashing, crooked shapes like shards of broken perception closed in around her. They severed the very essence of her and insinuated themselves into the gaps. Pauline screamed, the deep darkness swallowing her as her mind collapsed and her body fell to the ground.

Moments later, in the early morning sun, the thing that rode inside Pauline's body stood. It looked down the overgrown driveway that led to the main road. Dredging through Pauline's memories, it saw the town she had passed through to get to the house. It knew that a town meant people and people meant meat for others of its kind to come back, down through the angles from outside.

What had been Pauline set off, walking towards the town a few miles away. Its kindred were many, *and it would need a lot of meat.*

Trembler
By Lisa Marie Lopez

We are stranded on the side of Draybeck Road. I sit on the bumper of our broken down car, playing a game with myself: how many red cars can I count before the tow truck arrives. My father stands beside our car, constantly reminding my younger brother and me to stay clear from the traffic. Brett, standing off to the side playing video games on his phone, acts like he doesn't know us. Now that he's thirteen, he's become aloof and his vocabulary has diminished—particularly when dealing with my parents.

After counting seven red cars, I walk to the nearby Grab'N Go across the street. Inside, shelves brim over with candy bars, chips, and every cream-filled Hostess treat imaginable. I haven't eaten since breakfast. The sky is silvery now, with a faint crescent moon soon to charm the sky with its Halloween-like beauty. For me, the small convenience store with the washed out gray façade is paradise. Behind the counter, a guy, my age, glances up. Light brown hair swoops over his forehead with his every move. I imagine his free time is spent in a garage, rehearsing with his rock band.

Before I can decide what color his guitar is, I'm standing at the counter with an armful of snacks. I admire his hair and immediately hand brush mine, thinking about the breezy walk over. As he rings up my items, I read the name on his badge, Dylan. In my mind, I say our names together: Dylan and Cate. Has a nice ring to it, I think, and that's when the floor jolts under my feet. First I think it's a big rig barreling by, until I notice items on shelves are shaking. A few tiny bottles shelved behind the counter hit the floor and crash into a thousand pieces.

Dylan hollers earthquake, and I see panic rising in his eyes. He's waving me over, reaching for my hand. I climb up onto the counter top and leap over, taking the cash register and an empty coffee mug with me. Both hit the floor and shatter, just missing my head. We take shelter under the counter. Thoughts of my parents and my brother flash before me. My eyes mist. By the time I'm settled, the trembling has stopped.

"It was just a little trembler, probably no more than a 4 on the Richter's scale," Dylan says, his face relaxed now, beautiful. I sigh, somewhat relieved, finding comfort in his eyes. His hand is grasped in mine, warm and silky, and I wonder how long it's been there. A gentle squeeze brings me back to earth, melting my lips into a smile. I find my words.

"This wasn't anything like that 6.4 magnitude earthquake that hit southern California last month," I say, relieved now. My hand slips from his.

We stand up, careful not to step on the broken glass and liquids puddling the floor.

"No, good thing," he says.

We step outside. Immediately, I see my father and brother hustling over. When they approach us, I notice Brett is clinging onto my father's arm, wide-eyed with fear. He is no longer the surly thirteen-year-old who resents his parents, but six again, hardly more than a baby.

My father asks if I'm okay. I nod, staring into my brother's face. Tears have pooled Brett's eyes, and he flinches with every sound the night brings. Apparently, he's afraid of everything now: hostile cars, small animals rustling in bushes, the darkness of the night.

I wrap my arms around Brett, and assure him there's nothing to be afraid of. I feel Dylan's hand slip into mine again. Warm, inviting. I realize something greater than an earthquake has jolted my world.

End

Realities
Lisa Marie Lopez

She told herself it had to be a misunderstanding—his no show at Café Rosa. By now, they should have been bonding over caramel ribbon lattes. She didn't want to think about the rumors she'd heard at work. Rumors implying Stevie still talked to his ex, Sheena. Rumors implying Stevie had been seen locking lips with Sheena at Rob's Bar, just the day before. Instead, she remained in the café, watching life unfold through the window. Outside, cars honked and zigzagged across jam-packed lanes. Crowds of people poured through the glistening city sidewalks like children just let out of school. It was five p.m. on a Friday. The air was sultry, fervent with possibility. Maybe Stevie had been swept away with it all, or lost among the skyscrapers. Stupid to even consider, she thought. Stevie, with his wind-blown hair and pockets quietly packed with razor-sharp protection, had grown up a city boy.

"One small latte for Quinn," a young man's voice boomed from behind the counter. She moseyed up to the counter, stopping momentarily to gaze through the glass. Maple-dipped scones, lady fingers, and macarons in lovely pastels lined parchment paper. For a moment, she forgot she was sad.

Settling back at the corner table with her latte and a couple pastel macarons, Quinn resumed watching life through the window, hoping to see Stevie with his wind-blown hair, hustling over.

Instead, she saw something that made her insides sink. Her father was walking up the street, holding hands with a woman who was not her mother. A woman who was not her father's modest wife of twenty-one years. This woman, red lips and clattering heels, was a stranger to Quinn.

She sunk in her seat, hoping her father wouldn't look her way. She hadn't seen him in nearly a year. After the last mysterious woman, rumored to have been an employee at her father's job, he'd packed his bags and moved away, three towns west. Squinting, Quinn watched as they neared the window, both looking straight ahead. His face looked younger, gleaming with a crooked grin that displayed all his yellow, coffee-stained teeth. A goofy grin she hadn't seen in years, which now, only served as an annoyance. He was draped in a loose, loud turquoise collared shirt, hideous with a large paisley pattern. Since when had he gone for large paisleys and colors so loud? He'd always been a plain collared-shirt guy. Bland grays, businessman blues, clean whites. Nothing fancy, nothing daring.

She thought of Stevie now. She wondered if he was holding hands with Sheena—a girl whose face shone like the lit-up city. Her insides sunk deeper. She pushed her coffee aside. She wondered how her mother dealt with it all.

She watched as her father and the woman crossed the street, disappearing into another café—a café with a darker façade, and bold lettering. Café IZZY, it hollered. It didn't whisper like Café Rosa, with its pastel letters and pastel macarons. She would never know what lingered behind the bold red door, the kind of pastries and espressos they served. She would never know who the woman was holding her father's hand, or why Stevie hadn't shown.

End

The Compliance of Athena
By Matt Duggan

Several new cases of affluenza
have arrived in Olympia
see them carrying expensive shopping bags
surgically craved;
listen to the inner prison
inside one solitary eye -
in a city that keeps secrets
a dog - eat - dog sentiment.
shoplifters gather
around a new silver council bin,
swapping boxes of Nike
pocketing small bags of browns,
Everyone on the bus route
firmly transfixed on mobile phones,
miss the mugging on St Phillips Street
the crucifixion near Richland Common,
They tell us that our future
is a sunrise to a better world
when in reality it's nothing more
than a plastic sunset
placed from second-hand soil.

(Add product placement immediately)

Where the Windows Tilt in Winter
By Matt Duggan

It will rain for fifty days straight
once clouds be the mist on bridges
moving like dancing black & white tumbleweeds

We taste sounds and smell colors and see the scent of others
floating like morning dew inside of a flower –

Hyper beings caught inside the blue hour
when a man is catching words
outside conversations travel from the gutters –
call of the dead and lonely
the talk he'll never have - only hear
when windows tilt in winter;

We should have known
when the god of sleep is awake
his wings flapping in front of his face;
belly growing outwards – his beard greying forwards.

Midnight is a moon in full white beneath oak –
where inside palms of imaginary spectators
we shine stars in bright and muted song;
We are merely tourists dissembling yet another world
our portraits held inside wooden stares -
inside a locked house full of cracked glass.

A Cryptic Triptych
By Max Orkis

LINEWORK

Contorted out of contours
You come undone
Like braces, stasis, laces
You buckle, knot, and tie
Inflamed you flow like liquid gold
You splash like sperm
Bent out of shape, unshapely, porous
I blur and burn and bleed the border
Between the leapers unbound for
Cuffed knowledge, faith, and/or
Hope for an influx, ink
So I
Could spin or ebb
And break from outpours
Incontinent and longing for a chorus
In short, no one is one
Way out of line
Outside the box as you feel in such cases
You seep and spill and leak and you disorder
You soak evaporated and reformulated
An ocean paces
It brings its pebbles back into the fold
For it may pine
For them to penetrate it
To hop the fence of skin and gated skin
For why confine
Why
Web
When words are mated
In liaison or out, or in
You edge and angle and you mold
You cross and link
You zigzag as you worm
Into a thin unparallelled frontier
Or never straight or still or bold
You stand to be a nexus or a herm
A pore
It's neither there nor here
And nothing can ring more hardcore
Lines render nothing clear

TEXTURE

Great wall
So concrete
Every blemish, scar, dent
Every wrinkle, stain, speckle
Each fossilized bruise
Hard to outlive it
Canvas, mindscape, art
Protective patches of paint
Which strips
Patterns rough to the face
To the tips
Palms smooth and trace
To the beat
Which skips
No, not a mime
Cheek's warmer
Lips
Beads ooze
Sweat drips
Tappity-tap — rock
Knockity-knock
Hollow, this part
A perfect place
To hide
To install
But what? Maybe a heart?
But whose?
And here, brick, brick, brick, brick
Same-same — not a rhyme
But words are locked, glued with cement
Strung
Together they stick
Here, a lump
Taste, glide
Tongue
Lickety-lick
The tip catches, slips
Flick
No nips
Chains chime
Stretch, clang
Click
Pivot
Okay, low start
Push, feet
Then, bang, bone, bang
Against the constraint
Grow, grow, the bump
Vibration, loud, livid

Damn, that must have stung
The wall?
Former
Reason for rent
Not a mark, not a scratch, not a freckle
No chips
No longer dreading, hoping for the apocalypse
Do not faint
Lines link, interlace
Arms hang

FOCUS

A silence carries weight
It will depend
Oh, it will fluctuate
In rough proportion
To the amount of space
Between the source of heavy light
And the beholder's wide eye's white
It's blind point-blank and face-to-face
But an elusive dark distortion
Of an unreachable close whole
Just strokes or constellated dots
All in the distance
Between the surface and charcoal
Paper and graphite
Could it mean fate
Or the persistence
Of moths who mean to make a point? What's
The safe pull of a satellite
And say for instance
Earth
A question and a straight
Cold answer?
It's natural to orbit round, to gravitate
Towards meaning in the stalemate
What happens if these bodies mate?
What happens if hands fold the map?
What if the mouth does take the bait?
The eye won't see each dancer
Therefore the formula feels right
The choice to close the pulsing gap
Or stay in that one spot
This state
To seek the truth or to pretend
To make a move and blend
Despite
All reason to unite
Each twinkling dot
At arm's length and in earshot
As it appears the meaning's not
So out of mind if out of sight
In other words to separate
As with a colon or a dash
As with a lash
Or else to crash
To burn too hot
To peppered ash
Up close a silence tends to rend
Enough to fill a berth
The end

Love Before I Wake
By Nathan Noss

I felt loved. I felt safe. I felt happy in the comfort of his firm grasp around me. My eyes were closed, my breathing calm. I smiled at the pleasure of my company. I took in a breath of air. The aroma of his scent, warm as a candle, filled my lungs. With the smile everlasting on my face. I looked up into the face of my love.

His blue eyes lit the room. With his face square and perfect lips formed in the middle, he landed a kiss onto where my hair met my forehead. It was as gentle as a feather landing onto my crown. I took a hand of his into mine. My thumb rubbed the rouge skin of pumping vessels and cells, showing appreciation for the love he gave me.

I wished this moment would last forever. It felt like a dream, surreal. I was almost unable to grasp what reality this could be. How happy I really could be to feel loved like this. Could this really be real? My eyes questioned those of he who held me dearly.

"You know I love you," he answered back, satisfying my inquisitive worries.

"I love you too," I whispered back so only he could hear, adding softly to myself, more than you'll ever know.

He let another soft kiss meet my hairline. He left his lips lingering for a moment on my head, as if to plant the idea of love into it. Then with a hand rubbed the worries out of my arm, making sure it was planted into me well. With the whisper of an inhale, I felt him breathe my life into his lungs. Making sure my love reciprocated his.

"But I do have to go," he regretted to inform me.

I answered with a simple sigh, looking down. I lifted myself out of the nest of his warmth. I comforted myself with my own arms, wrapping them around where the spirit of his laid. With his forearm he lifted himself out of his resting position. He took a hand, reached out and used it to focus my face onto his.

"Hey, you'll see me again tomorrow," he said with little confidence, knowing it was not the same.

"I know," I smiled back at him. Then with a devious look, made a fist and tapped his shoulder with my knuckles. It was a pathetic excuse for a punch, but I replied nevertheless with certainty, "or I'll hunt you down and you'll never escape from me."

With a chuckle he flashed me a grin of pearly whites, handsome as ever. Oh, how I loved him. I leaned in for a kiss. Our lips connected, a spark giving flight to butterflies in my chest. It lasted for a moment or two of passion before I backed away from his face. I cupped his angelic cheekbone with my palm and locked eyes with his.

"You know I love you," I repeated to him.

"I know," he answered, cupping my cheeks in return.

We abandoned our positions, the couch a former skeleton of where we connected and hugged him for one last time.

"Text me when you're home?" I asked him in the crook of his ear.

"Always," he whispered back into mine.

Then he was gone. Door shut and locked, miles increasing between us. I got ready for bed, his scent lingering in the shadows of the darkened rooms. I crawled into my frozen bed and tried wrapping the covers around me. My sad attempt to mimic the comfort he had brought me. I missed him the moment before he even had to go. But for every second spent away, you appreciate every second you have.

My thoughts looked for my phone. I took it in hand from where it had been resting next to me. I brought its stiff body to light and tapped it's screen. A message had yet to bring it life. But regardless of waiting for that moment. I tapped open a connection I had to the one I loved.

"Goodnight," I typed with hearts and kisses, sending it across the miles to enlighten him.

I held the phone's structure in my hand, waiting for it to chirp a response I was waiting for. I grasp it like the skin of his body, waiting for life to pulse into it. I breathed in, and then out, creating the rhythm for sleep. I waited for him, missing him, thinking of him and dreaming of him. Falling gradually to sleep.

Then I woke up.

Zero Tolerance
By Phil Terman

A current event poem

1

If not filled
up with children
separated from parents
they soon will be—

these cages, chain-link:
a little water,
bags of chips, sleeping
on the floor, foil sheets
for blankets. No toys,
no books. All night
overhead lighting
for these *rapists,*
animals, invaders.

2

Dirty, scared, hungry,
no fruit, no vegetables,
no milk, flu epidemic, lice
infestation, no soap.

An 8-year old ordered
to care for a 2-year old.

3

If we go back
to our country,
they will kill us,

every last person,
even the dog.

A carpenter's son,
I was varnishing a chair
when they shot me
seven times: Narcos.
Two guys arrived
on a motorcycle.

They shot me seven times.
I'm blind in one eye.

Scars all the way up my arm.

Here we eat strange bread.
No money for meat.

We've asked
for asylum twenty times.
They always say:
"come back later."

Stay strong, a brother says.
Wherever your mother goes,
you go, too.

Frackin' Poem
By Phil Terman

Scarlet tanagers, thrushes, warblers, hawks,
spotted salamanders, skunk and possum,
all the invisible insects—

the native shrubs, the wild flowers,
all the trees cut down, the altered
light patterns, the shifting forest canopy,

all giving way for the gravel roads,
the trucks and tankers and dust,
hauling their chemical cocktails:

the methanol, the isopropyl alcohol,
the ethylene glycon, the crystalline silica,
and all the other toxins, according

to the Halliburton loophole, the industry
refuses to disclose, the toxins that cause
blurry vision, severe stomach cramps,

burning noses, swollen tongues, headaches,
hair loss, ear pressure, horses that won't leave the barn—
smell of sulphur, rotten egg, nail polish,

water burning out of faucets—
the heavy axles invading
across our farms, compacting the topsoil,

reducing plant growth, increasing
the runoff, the erosion like a fully-loaded
cement mixture hauling itself across a lawn

after a heavy rainfall, all the way
to our watersheds: the Ohio, the Susquehanna,
the Delaware, the Erie, the Genesee, the Potomac—

not to mention the 86, 000 miles of streams
and rivers, the 161, 445 acres of lakes,
the 403, 924 acres of wetlands—

the drilling through aquifers, the potential for leakage,
the uranium, the radioactive radon stored
in that black rock that is almost 400 million years old—

that shale that has survived from the Devonian age,
that stone of shelled swimmers, like squids,
of plant-like animals related to starfish called *sea lilies*,

that earth, that earth that once we contaminate,
we can never reclaim, that earth
that when we frack, we frack ourselves.

Just Another Fix
By Ray Van Horn, Jr.

1995. East side, Baltimore City.

The glisten of a Colt .45 revolver in my rearview mirror freaks me out before I hear the cussing and feel my Geo sedan rock on its axles.

Plastered sloppily upon long-standing bricks (erected in 1892, so the marker states) to my left are weather-battered advertisements for Arrested Development's album released last year, *Zingalamaduni.* The scabby holes in the color-washed paper make the jacket cover's ebony dancer appear leprous. As if the poor sales figures weren't insult enough, some racist prick has defaced the poor girl--no doubt having done that leg-cocked lurch many times before the image was settled upon—with a swastika. What the absolute fuck. Before acknowledging the sudden reality of my own predicament, I think of those jughead Neo Nazi skins we used to gang up on and toss out of the slam pit to the bouncers. Who invited *those* shitheads back to the party?

"It's cool! He's *alright!*"

Her name is Jenna and I refuse to know the rest. She twirls on more than just steel poles on Baltimore Street for a living. I was *warned* about Jenna. Never thought I'd be forced into seeing proof of that caveat.

In the mirror I also catch a shadow of the thrasher-punk hybrid I used to be. It was called crossover then. Gone is my sweaty shag, my silver hoop earring and my denim vest with all the band buttons and patches. I even outgrew my favorite G.B.H. and Nuclear Assault shirts. I miss that guy. After one stage dive too many, he leaped over to alternative, dark wave and industrial. The hair became a fabulous disaster in poor imitation of Martin Gore, an ill-advised frontwards follicle coif that never swung hot with black hair. I'd shocked it in a futile attempt to get laid by a Goth chick. Funny how that doofy, front-loaded mop attracted my bride-to-be, she being the furthest, bipolar track away from Goth as it gets.

My head's all close-cropped now, and I wear a goddamn suit and tie these days. I sold out, like I swore I'd never do, crashing around my bedroom like a one teen insurgence to the Subhumans a decade ago. I might not necessarily be in this predicament if I was *that guy,* because right now, I look like a post-collegiate version of *the man,* for Christ's sake. I have a terrifying vision of bloody phantasmagoria erupting out of my forehead, canvassing the windshield crimson, resulting in my slumped, exploded skull against the steering wheel. Hilariously, I hear an echo of MC Hammer and his floppy pants posse nattering *Let's turn...this mutha out...*

I don't dare laugh, though. Instead, an entire gust of disconcerted profanity whirls through my head, ending on "...I'm fucking dead..."

I clam up, because it's my only defense.

"Who *is* this motherfucker?" screams the first gangbanger who's jumped into the back of my car. A blue bandana around the dome marks him a Cripp. Glad I'm not wearing anything red, the way he seems intent on capping me. I *knew* I should've eaten my turkey sandwich for lunch instead of letting the girls at the office talk me into ordering pad thai with them. Residual curry coats the bile burning my throat this second, threatening to propel against the Plexiglas before my brains ever get that far.

"Goddamn Five-O," his companion snarls. He's wearing a blue Dodgers ball cap, assumedly a unifying gang color, since this is Orioles turf. His spit dashes my neck above the starched white collar. It scares more than repulses me, like he's salivating behind me, ready to gore my neck.

Together, they smell like they've been passing the city's longest-lasting spliff between them all afternoon. Gail's gonna think I've been getting high on the road. Because of that *one time* I did a joint on the set with the two grips on that indie film, *My Pariah,* which nobody voted for at The Charles Local Filmmakers' Festival. As mike boom operator, I'll take the rap for the scenes you have to strain to hear, since I'd been so stoned I soared around the actors. So stoned I'd outrageously banged on Gail's apartment door at one in the morning, declaring I was Robin Hood and demanding my Maid Marian bear me child that instant. She's given me shit about the incident ever since, and I'm pretty positive she's gonna serve me a balls-breaking playback to a hundred-plus in her reception speech.

Assuming I live that long to hear it.

Speaking of "shit," I say it to myself at least twenty times before making a silent vow to kiss the first safe ground I find if I make it out of the city without my blood left flung upon it.

"Undercover," the first Cripp says, but his tone settles a bit. "You vouch for this clown, Jenna? Never seen his punk ass before, so I gotta ask."

"He's *cool,"* Jenna affirms.

I can't believe the same junkie stripper who'd suckered me into this life-threatening chaos has just saved me.

When I first saw Jenna's raining track marks and ghoulish eyes, a tenant at my future father-in-law's roach café row home on Ellwood, I wanted to run out of there. I'd *hoped* she hadn't been at Italian Almost Dad's house, though Gail had warned me of the likelihood. I'd also hoped Italian Almost Dad (Vincent's his name, *of course*) would've kept me company, knowing Jenna would be hocking the first face she saw. Gail was late meeting us for dinner at Little Italy, my crummy luck. Thus Vincent took advantage and bailed on me, lured by a neighbor waving a circular advertising a sale on salami at the corner store. He told me he'd be back in an "easy twenty." Geezer *stunod* never could pass up a cheap deal, my worse luck. *Fongul,* Almost Dad.

I'd put my back to her when I'd first heard Jenna's screechy chirping. It hit somewhere between Jersey shore and the regional Baltimore 'hon speak. Her squawk was further jacked by a panic that made you want to shove her into a soundproof room locked from the outside. She must've called Vincent's name an easy dozen times, so much half the Old Country-relocated men of the neighborhood could've answered her.

My name being more American Mick, I cringed the second Jenna asked my back, "You're Brandon, aren't you? Thank *God* someone's here. Pleasure to meet ya. I'm gonna be *so late* for work I'll get docked from my tips. Can I impose upon you for a solid?"

I could shred my soft, stupid heart for getting me into this mess.

"Aight," the first Cripp says, sliding his gun into his Washington Bullets jacket. Relieved I'm not going to die yet, it dawns on me how that jacket's insane for a 94 degree August afternoon. All the easier to conceal, apparently. As long as it *is* concealed, that's a slam dunk for me.

I have no idea what possesses me, but knowing I'm out of immediate, if not overall danger, I drape my wrist overtop the steering wheel, tossing the world's worst low rider slouch. Street cool hardly passes inside of iron-pressed whitey banker's duds. Pathetic.

I send Jenna a glare she doesn't miss. She drops her head down a moment and the purported humiliation rings of a pose, since she quickly whirls around and chats up the Cripps. Her bare legs are bruised and gaunt from beneath the cheap red plastic skirt she has on, one that leaves a bony ass cheek hanging out. Her Bobby Brown shirt is twice her frame and I'm having trouble imagining her in action on a catwalk. I smell a disgusting waft of wisteria sodomized by tobacco upon her skin. My stomach hurts and this time, it's not from curry.

The Cripps tell me where to turn and I purposefully forget every street, every corner. Jenna audaciously turns Rush on my car radio to the local hip hop station. The voices blur inside my ears, even with SWV crooning alongside them. All I want is to get this over with, since I'm now committed to helping this skank score. I think of the only other girl I ever used the word "skank" around, Penny Allen. Her mouth was far looser than her thighs, and she'd punched me a good one in the gut for dropping the "skank" tag on her. In Jenna's case, I'm pretty sure I've hit the mark.

I stop when my uninvited backseat guests tell me to, but I'm so numb I haven't seen this set of guys climb out of my car and two new guys take their place.

This time, there's no shouting, no threats, no guns waving at me. I've cleared the first wave of this Cripp crew, and, whack me with a size 10 leather loafer, I'm "in." As we drive on, I take strange comfort by the head bobbing of the new arrivals and their mercifully calm "turn here's."

I could piss myself every time we pass any cops, but they're either idling in their patrol cars or chattering amongst themselves in a cluster. Whether or not they're aware this street is the fourth of six legs leading to a drug house, I'll never know. Each stop we clear with new pushers makes me lose faith I'm gonna live, at the same time making me worry the *real* undercover's about to jump in and slap cuffs on me after conking me with a Glock handle.

I get *really* scared on the sixth stop.

"Leave it running," one of the sixth duo of Cripps tells me as he and Jenna get out of my car. I'm tempted to burn all the tread I have left in a grand escape, even knowing my left front tire is dire need of replacement.

To hell with Jenna, let her fend for herself from here, I tell myself, adding, *I hope they tip your scrawny, lying butt in quarters tonight.*

That not me, though, and there's the other Cripp keeping me company. Or is he guarding me?

"Wass your name, dawg?" he asks casually, drawling the end of his query. He catches me off-guard, since nobody's asked me for my name the entire time until now.

"Greg," I lie, somehow avoiding a full stutter.

"Cool," he says to me without offering me his name back. Fine by me, at this point. The less I know...

Yet I *do* know two things. This guy is young and his jaw's been broken, maybe twice. Worse, the kid's still young enough to break his parents' hearts. That being said, he gives me my first and only laugh on this hell ride by muttering, "Hotter than my motherfucking nut sack out there." I think of Coolio's perverse rap about leaving his hand affixed to the same sweaty anatomy, a total white collar hit in the office.

I'll give her this much; Jenna's back in the car by the time we settle down our laughter. The junior Cripp gets out and tells us both to have a good rest of our day with far less gangsta to his parting words. Thankfully, nobody else enters the rear of the Geo.

"Go," Jenna says quietly. When we're blocks away, she adds, *"Thank you,* you're so cool."

"Forget the thanks," I fume. I look at her purse, knowing whatever she bought and would later blast her brains out with whatever is stashed in there. It amplifies my anger.

"I'd like to show you my gratitude," she says, resting her hand on my thigh. Even through navy dress slacks, I can feel the leathery skin and peeling calluses. "Will a knobber on the house settle it?"

"I don't think so," I growl, lifting her emaciated hand and dropping it to her side of the car. "Gail, my fiancée, wouldn't appreciate it too much."

"She doesn't have to know," Jenna says, and it's more hateful than her lie which had nearly gotten me killed.

"Is that a fact?" I snarl at her. I can't believe how quickly we're back at Vincent's place, and the smug old bastard is on the stoop, waving to us with his arm slung around his daughter, as if daring me to come claim her. My biggest concern right now is Jenna, though, and the quicker I'm rid of her, the quicker I'll claim my bride. *Rip* her from her dud of a dad if I have to. "How about asking *her* opinion?"

"You're a good guy, Brandon," Jenna tells me with a sigh before climbing out of my car. Using the same annoying squeak, she toodles over to Vincent and pecks him on the cheek before patting Gail on the shoulder in a way that creeps me out. Gail will be creeped too, once I have the stones to retell this event. "Gotta jet, Vinnie! My bus'll be here in ten minutes. Pleasure to meet ya, Vinnie's daughter!"

Gail is in my arms and planting a conservative, if full-puckered kiss. She always gets leery with her father watching us and I wonder if it'll always be that way. Right now, it doesn't matter, because I feel guilty, moreover *filthy,* by the mere gall of Jenna's proposal and her willingness to put me, a stranger, in harm's way.

I'm alive, but I feel like I should've died like Arrested Development's recent unit sales, a pale shade behind *3 Years, 5 Months and 2 Days in the Life Of...* Exactly the amount of time I felt like I'd been shuttling Jenna to get her fix.

"Canolis at Vaccaro's for desert, just saying," Gail tells me, rubbing my chest.

"Yeah," I mutter, soaking the heat from Gail's hand. Even in this humidity, I'd gone cold a moment. "Absolutely. Vaccaro's. You got it."

Jenna's already turned the corner up Fayette. Italian Almost Dad looks at me with a knowing smile. I want to flip him off right there, in front of his daughter.

I can hear Al Jourgensen's take on this, I seethe to myself. *Never trust a junkie.*

Weighed Down
By RJ Robertson-DeGraaf

183.4 lbs

I am utterly atrocious at flirting.

As I waited for the rest of my hallmates to file into the study lounge, I picked small pieces of pleather off my sweaty underarm. A baby-faced freshman shimmied between my chair and a coffee table stacked with welcome pamphlets. I leaned back, partly to give him more space, and partly to get my nose as far away from the kid's sweat soaked tank as possible.

The RA looked so excited to give his spiel I thought the poor guy would have an aneurism if the hall director didn't give him the go-ahead in the next few minutes, but only a dozen of the supposed twenty five people on our floor sat around waiting for the meeting to start. A few stragglers filed in, unapologetic for their tardiness. Among them was the most beautiful man I'd ever seen.

His face looked like it had been sculpted by a Renaissance artist with a jawline so sharp it should've been considered a blade. His millennial librarian style gave the impression that he was as straight as a circle, while his man bun and slight stubble surely made panties drop. He couldn't have been taller than 6 feet, barely an inch taller than me, but his fit, beanpole frame put him solidly in the 'otter' category. As per usual, I wasn't sure whether I wanted to be him or fuck him.

He crossed the room and placed himself on the empty sofa next to me, close enough that I could've nonchalantly brushed my hand against his if I wasn't so chickenshit. I did my darndest to control my heart rate, but it did little to stop it from playing a drum solo against my sternum. My mind flitted through every shitty pickup line horny guys on Tinder had ever sent my way, but they either seemed too rehearsed or an immensely skeevy phrase to say to a stranger.

The RA motioned for us to direct our attention to him and proceeded to rattle off the incredibly obvious rules that were posted on flyers every few feet throughout the building. He rambled on about quiet hours and banned objects for a few minutes before assigning an infantile 'get-to-know' you game and allowed us to pair off. Before the sweaty freshman had a chance to make purposeful eye contact, I turned to the Adonis on my left and tilted my head to the side, raising one eyebrow in an expression meaning "partners?" He nodded and I shifted forward in my seat, my skin peeling off the pleather armchair with a wet scraping sound.

Before my brain had decided between 'how are you?' and 'what's your name?' my mouth blurted out, "What are you?"

He laughed out a confused, "What now?"

Luckily, my mind had caught up and formulated a smooth reply to make up for its earlier mistake.

"A greek god or an angel?" I managed with a straight face, "You're far too handsome to just be human."

"Lol, I'm Alex and I'm just a run-of-the-mill starving college student," he blushed.

"Damn. I was really hoping for vampire."

"Well what are you: wizard or elf?" he asked, gesturing to my Lord of the Rings tank top.

"Ah, I see what you did there. I am James: Prince of Mirkwood," I said. Immediately, my stomach twisted with embarrassment. "Sorry, I'm a super nerd."

"Nah, don't apologize. Having passions is cool as fuck."

"Alright, just one more thing before we're done," the RA interrupted. He went off on a long tangent about participation requirements and room checks, gesticulating so wildly with his hands he nearly slapped a girl sitting on the floor next to him. I kept glancing over at Alex but his gaze was fixed on the speaker. When the sermon was finally concluded, everyone rose to leave. I gathered every ounce of bravery I had, which didn't amount to much, and drew in a breath.

"Wanna go out sometime?" I blurted. Alex's eyebrows twitched for a moment and his smile faded.

"Oh, I'm actually gay. But you seem nice... maybe I'll see you around, somewhere."

I stood stunned for a moment, my breathing growing angrier as he walked out the door. I could feel my face redden as I blinked back tears before they could form. I clenched the pamphlet in my fist and speed-walked down the hall. I quickened my step as a few tears leaked out, and fumbled putting my key in the door before shoving it open.

My breath came in ragged bursts, the way a toddler inhales after bawling, but hardly any tears fell down my cheeks. I was so stupid and infantile, crying over something that had happened a thousand times before, but in this new environment, the thought of everyone still seeing the chubby, awkward girl I'd tried to run from, was more devestating than any transphobic crap bigots could throw at me. I looked into a full-length mirror hanging on the bathroom door and saw what they saw: a pretender. The carefully selected boyish haircut couldn't hide my soft jawline or dainty features. My eyelashes held the appearance of mascara, though no makeup had touched my face in years. My tank barely covered the binder and left nothing to the imagination. Though it compressed them, my binder still didn't eliminate the 'breast bump' that usually denoted to others that I was in fact, born female, and my overexaggerated curves didn't help. Nothing in my reflection gave any indication I was male and, despite having fought so hard to get on testosterone last month, my voice was still well within the soprano range. *You're a fraud and everyone knows it.*

163.8 lbs

The garbage truck might as well have been playing shot put with the racket it made every other morning. I flipped off the window, even though the blinds were down. I'd turned off my Friday alarm, intending to skip my bullshit exercise class in favor of sleeping, but here I was, up at the crack of dawn anyways. I probably should've taken this as a sign that I should attend the courses my Dad had paid so much for, but I couldn't drag myself out of bed to listen to drivel I'd learned in every PE class since elementary school.

I patted the blankets around my waist, feeling for my phone. It was dangling off the edge of the mattress, held up by the power cord. I delicately reeled it in and pressed my thumb to the home button. The prospect of opening Tinder to find the same four matches still hadn't messaged back was too much to deal with before nine am, so I flipped through apps until I found Tumblr. 18 notifications. Either someone *really* liked my page or I had a couple new followers. I hit the 'activity' button to find the same emaciated avatar on every notification. For all I knew, the picture of collarbones on my page and the picture of ribs that went with my new obsess-ee's username came from the same guy. Almost every thinspo picture had been recycled a couple dozen times on different mood boards and collections, reblogged and liked by a few hundred accounts that all followed one another. My dash consisted of half-naked Instagram models and 'tips' on how to cut calories with the odd melodramatic song lyric photoshopped over a dark landscape and depressing meme sprinkled in.

By the time my class would've started I'd been scrolling for an hour and a half, absorbing vaguely correct nutrition information and tricks for suppressing my appetite. I glanced at the clock again and the gnawing feeling of 'I should be doing something productive' settled in its usual spot in my chest. I kicked off my covers and jumped to my feet, downing half a can of diet Coke and an antidepressant. I slipped into clean clothes, coating my armpits and underboob in antiperspirant spray. I grabbed a random sock from the floor and shoved my feet into already-tied tennis shoes, the backs caving under my heels.

My keys and ID in hand, I made my way towards one of the three spots within a quarter mile of my dorm building where I was ever able to park my car. The air was chilly for so early in

October and stung as it whipped against my face. Though it'd been sitting in direct sunlight, the air inside my car was brisk, and stank of old McDonalds fries. I turned the key in the ignition and idled for a moment, selecting a playlist to blast for the twenty minute drive. I pulled out of the parking lot, taking turns faster than was probably safe, and was off campus in two minutes. I weaved around lazy drivers and idiots too anxious of being pulled over to break the speed limit, turning the journey into a sixteen minute one. There were only three other cars parked around the playground and a couple pairs of tykes swinging or hanging from the jungle gym. I'd have the path to myself for the most part.

I turned up my music and burrowed my hands deep in my hoodie pockets. The red beanie I'd grabbed from my backseat could probably be seen from space but it kept my ears warm enough to justify wearing it. The leaves over the hiking trail were halfway to the brilliant crimson fall is famous for and some threatened to fly off with every gust of wind blowing past. My shoes tapped the concrete to the "hey-ya oo hey" of Centuries, moving my body to the beat of whatever emo anthem blared through my headphones. Despite the modern music, I imagined myself on a DnD style journey, off to save a village from goblins or some shit.

Every so often I'd pass a mile marker, silently calculating how far I'd have to go before I could have whatever craving popped to the front of my thoughts. Pizza, tacos, turkey sliders, brownies dipped in peanut butter, blueberry pancakes in the shape of Mickey Mouse, and Mom's seven layer bean dip scooped out of the pan with tortilla chips. Every food I'd dreamed up in my mind-numbing gen ed courses. Caramel popcorn, Grandma's baked ziti, baked beans with cut up hot dogs, and every dessert under the sun. My stomach growled as I wiped drool from the corner of my mouth. *Don't listen to that pathetic whiner. You don't need food, you just want it.*

The path ended at an outlook over the river that ran alongside the length of the trail. Water lapped at the edges of the wooden perch, weeks of unrelenting rain raised the water level past its normal bounds. Moss covered stones and overgrown roots reached down into the stream, disappearing into the murky sludge. It looked gray in the midst of the yellowing landscape. In the half dozen times I'd visited since moving to campus, the river had lost its vibrancy, draining color from the surrounding forest.

I turned back to the trail, skipping to the next track on my phone, and began the four mile walk back to my car.

d

146.0 lbs

The words just wouldn't come. I sat in the same corner of the library I'd been for hours. Sunset came and went while I sat staring at the cursor blink in a blank document. Every time some eloquent idea formed in my head my fingers sprang into action, attempting to jot down the concept before it evaporated. To my left the textbook laid open to a page I hadn't so much as glanced at since sitting down. The computer screen drifted in and out of focus, either due to exhaustion or lack of food.

My only company stood across the floor scrawling code on a whiteboard. One member of their study group was sprawled on a couch, snoring happily. My own eyelids grew heavy. What a lucky bastard, a nap sounded amazing. Could I even pass without this paper? It'd be stupid to retake such a basic class over one bad weekend but my thoughts stagnated, the last coherent notion circling the drain. Fuck it. I threw my textbook into my backpack and pushed back from the desk so forcefully the chair rolled back a couple yards, slamming into a table. *Whatever, just fucking leave it.*

The muted throbbing in my stomach intensified as I tore past the automatic doors. In the glass, my hair resembled a bird's nest with clear outlines of hands on each side where my fingers had burrowed into my scalp. The biting winter air would've stung my face if it hadn't been hot with anger and frustration.

I'd done well enough on the midterm that the final grade would probably be around seventy percent. That was passing, right? Even if it wasn't, one failed class wasn't enough to put me on academic probation. Might fuck up my chances at a scholarship, but Dad'd be happy to spend his inheritance on his little baby's higher education. Always had been happy to throw money at anything he thought might win my affection. Even after I'd picked him in the custody debate, a check had always been his preferred method of showing love.

I took a meandering path back to my dorm, going around as many halls and parking lots as I could without getting lost. Campus was always dead Sunday nights, but even the rabbits and deer that usually grazed by the pond had hidden themselves away. The only morons still wandering the sidewalks at midnight were me and a gaggle of drunk girls staggering their way up the hill towards the apartments behind me. When they were a few feet away, a particularly inebriated young woman lurched forward to pet my face.

"Where are you all by yourrrrself?" she slurred. "You shouldn't go alone to…"

I waited a beat but that seemed to be the end of her statement. She clasped my chin in a way that forced eye contact between us. Her face held such a sincere look of concern, I almost laughed.

"Just going to Johnson Hall. I'll be fine. You just make sure you get back safe." I caught her before she could collapse into me. Her friends tried to hurry her away but none of them were sober enough to carry her weight. They stumbled towards the buildings, my drunk buddy trailing slightly behind.

"Be safe. We ladies gotta stick together." she called after me.

I pressed my palm to my eye, chuckling. "Pfft heh. All the shit I've been doing doesn't even matter."

I made every wrong turn, exploring winding paths that lead further from where I was supposed to be, muttering obscenities at dead trees. "Fuck my 8am class, fuck my stupid fucking essay, fuck all these goddamn wastes of my time."

I kept going until I could no longer stand the sting working its way up my fingers or my backpack straps rubbing grooves into my shoulders. Eventually, I would have to go to bed; might as well do it before I got frostbite.

I signed into Johnson Hall and stood over the radiator blasting heat at the entrance in an attempt to thaw my hands. When I could finally feel my fingertips again, I started towards the staircase but before I made it to the door my stomach let loose a howl that could've been heard across campus. Without thinking, I turned to the vending machine and started swiping my card, buying any and everything that sounded vaguely appetizing. My backpack was filled in minutes, but I didn't quit punching buttons until every pocket on my person was bursting with junk food. I scurried upstairs and was slumped over on my bed shoveling snacks into my gullet before my thoughts could catch up.

STOP, what are you doing?! The food kept coming. I didn't even taste half of what was swallowed. My jaw ached from frantic chewing but nothing slowed until the last package was emptied of every crumb. *Now look what you've done, you pig. This is where giving in gets you.* Every inch of my bedding was covered in wrappers and dropped bits of sweets. It looked like a hurricane had ripped through the room.

Getting up to run over to the bathroom brought with it acid reflux so strong I was sure something must've torn. I doubled over in the doorway, awaiting a gap in the burning in which to stand and retrieve a water bottle. The hunched creature that stared back at me in the mirror hanging from the door hardly seemed real. Her stomach was so distended it could've held twins, and her face was twisted in a horrible grimace that could turn men to stone. She seemed like the type of horror movie monster Stephen King would dream up: a pale malformed thing that hunted children in the dead of night. *You're hideous.*

When I was able to crawl my way back to my bed, I abandoned any thought of relief. *You deserve this. Failure.* I stood to rip the *Last Airbender* poster down from my wall, not even wanting cartoon eyes to witness the appalling state of my room. I burrowed into my pile of garbage and soaked my pillow with tears until I finally drifted off to sleep.

134.9 lbs

My phone buzzed again. Probably another text from my mother wondering if she should be expecting me for the holidays. The thought of having to wolf down such a massive feast in front of so many people made me more nauseous than the prospect of the eight hour flight I'd have to take to get there and back. If Mom wanted to spend her Thanksgiving with me, she shouldn't have packed up and left to start her new 'perfect' family. *You're not good enough for her. She has a real son now.*

The phone lit up with a picture of my mother's face. We had the same grey eyes and upturned nose, but hers suited her face. She could've been a model; the kind of beautiful face that makes you want a fifth 'live, love, laugh' picture frame so you can pretend you're as happy as the face on the other side of the glass. I let her go to voicemail.

Three missed calls. After a fourth I'd probably feel guilty enough to formulate some excuse to explain my absence, but I'd never be brave enough to tell her I didn't want to see her.

I slipped my feet into loafers and left the dorm room, my phone still on the desk. I locked the door, trying to keep the image of myself dressed up in my Sunday best next to the step-siblings I'd maybe said a handful of words to in just as many years stuffed away in the bedroom. It didn't work. I tried to shake the thoughts from my brain and nearly ran into a student coming up the stairs. I knocked a stack of papers out of his hands and they scattered in every direction.

"Oh god, I'm so sorry." I scrambled to pick up as many sheets as I could before the water tracked into the building by boots could ruin his work.

"No no, it's fine. I was bringing these to the recycling bin anyway." He looked up and the hood that'd been covering his face fell back. It was my beautiful hipster librarian, Alex. "I need to watch where I'm going, almost killed you."

"It was my fault, sorry."

"Oh, it's you. Prince of the woods, right?" he smiled. "Haven't seen you since like the first month of classes."

"Yeah, I'm a umm... bit of an introvert." I kept collecting his papers to avoid ogling his gorgeous body. I could see his biceps bulging through his thin winter jacket. He really could've been a statue carved by Michelangelo.

"Could've fooled me. I never forgot when you called me a god that first day. I'm pretty sure it's the nicest fucking thing anyone's ever said to me."

"Well it's not unwarranted. You're gorgeous," I said, handing him the stack of papers I'd gathered from the floor. "I uh... think some of these are wet."

He shifted around the binders and notebooks held in his arms, and tried to reach for the pile without dropping anything. "Would you mind carrying them to the trash with me? I don't have enough arms for all this."

We climbed in awkward silence for a few moments, his shoes squeaking out a rhythm that reminded me of High School Musical. I nearly started humming the words before Alex spoke, interrupting my internal musical number.

"Sorry if I offended you when we met. I didn't know you were a dude."

"It's fine. Happens all the time."

"I'm still sorry about it, I kinda regret not taking you up on that date."

I blushed as I opened the door to our floor for him. "Oh?"

"It's true. You're pretty fucking hot for a freshman." He dropped his armful of garbage into the trash can at the end of our hall. "Do you--I mean, are you going to see family or anything next week?"

"No."

"Want to come to my room and chill? I've got some edibles and an HBO subscription."

"Oooo tempting. I just- I didn't think you'd...be interested in- what I've got going on down here." I gestured to my crotch with my free hand.

"Are you a bottom?"

I nodded.

"Then I'm interested." He took the last of the papers from my arms and dumped them into the trash. "Let me make up for being a dickhead."

He leaned forward, closing his eyes. In my head, I played out a soap opera love scene where as we watched a movie our hands brushed one another's, our eyes met, and we were overcome by our attraction. Passionate making out that lead to us removing our shirts as the camera panned away so the show could keep its PG rating.

Just imagining his lips against me made my heart race. Our hands wrapped around one another's, his body pressed against mine. My body. Even if anything ever made it that far, how could I ever subject him to the grotesqueness that was hidden under my clothes?

"I uh," my hands trembled. "I don't..."

I never finished my sentence. I turned and raced down the flights of stairs. *Stupid, stupid, stupid. You're finally good enough to trick someone into liking you, and you've blown it. Moron.* When I got out of the building, I broke into a run. Every awkward interaction I'd ever had bubbled to the surface of my thoughts until my brain felt like a boiling, stinking mess of failed conversations. My calves burned as my legs gained momentum. Buildings and trees blurred into one large wall of color and shapes. A week long fast left nothing for my body to pull energy from, but I sprinted until my lungs were on the brink of exploding. I gasped for air, my chest pressing against the binder that hung from my chest with every inhale.

Alex's words echoed through my head, looping and slurring together until they were too garbled to understand. How could I ever look him in the eye again? He was yet another reason not to come back next semester.

118.2 lbs

I shot up; a hard feat while lying on my stomach, my head underneath two pillows. The blankets had twisted around my legs, effectively immobilizing them, while my headphones threatened to strangle me. Before I could detangle myself, the rustling started again. Not an unfamiliar noise this early, but much closer to my mattress than they'd ever dared come before. I squinted, hoping to spot a rodent silhouette in the dim green glow from my smoke detector, but the room was nearly as dark as the backs of my eyelids. The distinct plastic crinkling of a chip bag followed by distressed squealing brought my attention to my nightstand. I fumbled my fingers across the base of my bedside lamp, knocking something off the nightstand before finding the switch.

My eyes were slow to adjust to the sudden brightness but I could make out a tiny dark figure darting across the carpet. The squealing hadn't stopped but had become so much quieter after turning the light on that my groggy brain couldn't find its source.

"Great to be home," I whispered sarcastically. Across the room, I could make out the hour hand between three and four, though the clock hung lopsided from the single nail in the wall. It could've been any time between midnight and four am.

"Too early for this shit," I muttered, pulling my comforters over my head. My eyes were so warm and heavy that what little lamp light that peaked through the fabric wasn't enough to keep me awake.

When I was eventually able to pry my crusted eyes open, sunlight streamed in through the two inch gap between the top of the window and the curtain rod. My phone had worked its way under my left shoulder with my earbuds creeping under my sweatshirt. My eleven am alarm buzzed, sending a strange vibrating sensation down my back.

As I fully emerged from my blanket cocoon, a heavy scent of decay permeated the usual rotten, molding food smell that lingered in my room. I yearned to investigate but the thought of finding a little dead mouse body made me shudder.

I jumped off the bed, careful to avoid the sea of trash surrounding it. Crumpled chip bags covered layers of half-empty nugget boxes and fruit snack wrappers. Weights peeked out from under the corner of the bedpost and pellets of mouse poop were scattered amongst jelly beans and tissues filled with chewed mounds. I cleared the piles, landing in one of the few clear spots of carpet. I could feel the blood leaving my head, draining down my long limbs to the ice blocks I called my feet, nearly passing out as my vision narrowed. My knees locked, holding me in place as the tension between my temples slowly faded.

Once I was certain I could walk without losing consciousness, I paraded down the path of rugs that covered the water stained concrete floor outside my bedroom. Before I'd even reached the basement bathroom my sweatshirt and sports bra were off. I peed like a racehorse and cleaned up without pulling back on my boxers.

The vigorous drying took longer than washing my hands had. Needed to be thorough so that any leftover water didn't show up on the scale. I pressed the power button with my big toe and waited for the scale to light up and zero out. Aggressively exhaling, I stepped on.

Fuck. Not even half a pound less than yesterday.

I glared at the blob in the mirror. Thunder thighs painted with pale white lines, some the product of puberty and others a crosshatch of jagged scars. What had once been an hourglass figure was lumpy and seemed to dart in and out at random. The stomach made up for its lack of definition in excessive amounts of dark, rough hair. Though the bottom ribs were just visible, the rest of the torso was ruined by two massive lumps that sagged uselessly mid-chest. A long, giraffe neck ended in a double chin that hid any semblance of a jawline. Cheeks caked with acne and peach fuzz drooped below under-eye bags so dark they could be mistaken for bruises. The whole reflection was repulsive.

I straightened, pulling at the skin under my neck, the love handles at my sides, and the flab that coated my abdomen. When my phone started vibrating the noon alarm, my upper body was covered in irritated red splotches. Giving the mirror a last disgusted look, I grabbed a toothbrush and leaned over the toilet. After a couple of gags, the bowl was filled with stomach acid. I flushed, pulled on my boxers, and gave my mouth a quick rinse before reluctantly heading back down the hall towards the stench.

It took forty minutes of digging through food wrappers, half-empty diet coke cans, and bags of spat out candy before I found the mouse's final resting place. The poor thing looked vacuum sealed in a dollar store bag, it's fur covered in bits of peppermint and caramel. I haltingly wrapped the suffocated corpse in two other plastic bags, pausing to dry heave over my mattress.

I threw back my regular breakfast of three antidepressants and a laxative before sloppily applying deodorant and squeezing into a stained binder. The only clean clothes left were tucked away in a dresser drawer, covered in mouse shit. I scooped up as many abandoned socks and sweatpants as my shaking arms could hold, and dashed for the stairs, trailing shorts behind me. I was halfway across the kitchen before I heard Dad's voice.

"Meg?" Sitting in his recliner, Dad was still in his checkered pajama pants I'd bought for his birthday. He stared at me with a mix of amusement and confusion before realizing what he'd called me. "I mean James. Sorry...sorry-I, sorry."

"Why aren't you at work?"

"I get a Christmas break too, doofus. Also, I have a load in-" his smile dropped. I followed his gaze to my bare arms. "What're you-"

Before he could finish his thought, I took three massive steps, crossing the remaining distance to the laundry room and slammed the door shut behind me. I let my laundry fall to the floor and rummaged through the mess for the bulkiest items.

"Honey?"

I didn't respond. I pulled some old middle school track pants on. All my shirts reeked of BO but I whipped the dryer open and rummaged through Dad's things, stuffing my head through one of his sweaters seconds before he burst in. We just stared at each other. I fixed my gaze on his stubble, unsure of what might be looking back at me if I met his eyes. I flinched as he grabbed my wrist and yanked up the sleeve.

"How did- you're just skin and bones my love," his voice cracked. I twisted my arm out of his grasp and darted past him, easily sliding between his bulky frame and the door. I heard him call out something as I sprinted down the stairs, taking them two at a time, but my heart was racing too loudly to make out the words.

I flung the door closed and locked it for good measure but no footsteps followed me. He had to be pissed, or worse disappointed. *You're an adult, you don't need his approval.* I paced the length of the basement, playing Fur Elise with my thumb and forefinger on my collarbones. He knew. Even without looking him in the eyes, I'd seen his expression. He'd probably call a therapist or send me across the state for some inpatient counseling.

He would make me eat.

My pacing grew to a jog. Every lap around the basement would have to be 50 steps, every 2,000 burned 100 calories. 10,000 steps could burn a small dinner.

I jogged until my lungs began burning with every breath. The rhythmic whooshing of my pulse drowned out the sound of heavy panting, and my eyes pulsed with every heartbeat. I grabbed my phone from under the pillow but my hands shook too violently to draw the password pattern.

I hadn't had hunger pains in days, but my stomach spasmed in my abdomen, sending up bursts of gas that tasted like the peppermint I'd allowed myself yesterday. For an agonizing moment, I could feel my entire digestive system burning. *This will pass, you're fine.* Gradually, the pain faded to a dull ache behind my belly-button. I slowly lowered myself onto my bed. My limbs were so heavy with exhaustion I couldn't be sure I'd ever get back up. My thoughts that normally raced constantly, felt as though they were trudging through mud, fighting to reach the front of my mind, but far enough out of reach that I couldn't quite grasp them.

The last thing I could piece together before drifting into unconsciousness was: *If this is how I die, so be it.*

109.1 lbs

Dad scooped heapfuls of mashed potatoes onto my plate. He didn't trust me anymore.

The steam rising off the pot roast mixed with the smell of the rotting pine tree in our living room. A stupid purchase, done purely out of spite for my mother and all the years she had hauled up a fake Christmas tree from a box in the basement, and spent all day putting her ornament collection on it. If last year was any indication of how this one would go, the real tree would sit wilting in the corner until well past Easter, shedding pine needles that were never fully removed from the carpet.

A dinner plate piled with peas, potatoes, and pot roast was placed in front of me. My favorites. Maybe, since it was a new year I could have some- *No. Don't be weak.* I grabbed my fork, keenly aware of my dad's eyes on me. Shaking, I cut the chunks of beef into minuscule pieces, smearing the thick broth around in an attempt to make it look like I'd eaten more. I brought the first bit to my lips. *Stop you fucking failure.* I fought to keep my fork from getting to my mouth, my forearm trembling with effort. I could feel Dad's eyes burning a hole in the side of my head. He cleared his throat expectantly. I thrust the food into my mouth, chewing quickly. Out of the corner of my eye I saw Dad begin cutting his own meal. I swallowed hard and stabbed another fragment of beef, forcing it past my lips before any part of me could protest.

Much of the dinner passed in the same fashion, hurried tiny bites followed by moving the remaining food around the plate, spreading it thin. The air was thick with unspoken hostility and the sound of forks scraping ceramic dishes. The only breaks in the heavy silence were occasional sighs from my father that didn't lead to conversation. After the fifth sigh, I snapped.

"What?" My voice came out louder than I meant it to. I sunk into myself, unable to take back my words.

"I just... we can't keep going like this." He looked at me over the rim of his glasses. "You're wasting away Meg."

I didn't correct him. Instead, I grabbed my plate and rose. What was left of my dinner was tipped into the trash, my plate set in the sink. I stormed past him without a word and crossed the kitchen.

"Wait, please. I just want-" His plea was cut off by my feet thudding down the steps. "Come back Jam-" The basement door slammed. He wouldn't come down but I still locked the door behind me.

I sprinted down the hall, skidding into the bathroom. I tore open the cupboard under the sink and threw aside bottles of cleaner, fumbling for the decade old bottle of ipecac I'd squirreled away. I ripped the lid off and tipped it back, practically inhaling the syrup. I pulled the bottle from my lips and recapped it. Standing over the toilet, I could feel my stomach contents bubbling. I knelt as the heaving started, my knees pressed against the bottom of the bowl.

Wave after wave of nausea wracked my body long after the last of the pot roast had been flushed away. I had no way of knowing how much time was spent hugging the sides of the toilet. When the convulsions subsided and the blaze in my throat dulled enough to tolerate, I hobbled my way to my bedroom. The clock swayed, blurring at the edges. It could've been eight or nine. The numbers melted into one another, every dash extending to past the edges of the rim, bleeding into the paint on the wall.

It's still there, weighing you down. Burn it all off. I yearned to lay down and let the room spin around me, but my feet carried me towards the stairs. I opened the door as quietly as the hinges would allow to find every light upstairs off. The stairs danced in front of me, pulsing with my vision. I crawled up, avoiding the parts that groaned under any weight, and silently slipped the pair of shoes nearest the door onto my aching feet. Turning the bolt, I inched the door open until I could squeeze between it and the doorframe. I left it slightly ajar so it couldn't lock and braced for the frigid air.

The neighborhood was still. At the edge of our driveway, a street light flickered sporadically. My heart matched its uneven pattern. I grabbed my wrist, wrapping my thumb and middle finger around it and steadied my breathing. My feet followed the sidewalk while I moved my hand up my left arm, not breaking the circle until it met my elbow. *You're in control. Safe.*

The cloudy night sky left me little light to navigate with and the further I got from houses the more spaced out street lights became. When moonlight did break through, it lit the road for a precious few seconds before disappearing again, giving me glimpses of the path I was taking. At times, the road would sway under my feet and begin twisting into the sky. It became rare that I could tell which direction I was facing or even whether I was standing or laying flat on my back, but I couldn't stop.

The world faded behind a wall of static, coming back in a painting of disconnected dots. My stomach did backflips through my abdomen and sent a white hot spurt of acid to my throat; my nostrils burned as I spat it out onto the base of a street sign. *You're so close. You can't quit, not again.* The sidewalk turned away from the road, up a steep incline to a bridge overlooking the street. Agonizing pain crept up the back of my skull, threatening to split it in half. At the top of the hill, my legs gave out. I could no longer feel anything below my knee except for a chill that clung to my bones. I looked out through the bars of the guardrail at the street, my heart pounding against my sternum.

With effort, I pulled my legs up over the railing, my feet dangling over the three story drop onto the street below. My knuckles white with effort from gripping the handrail behind me, I leaned over the empty air. Legs shaking, I managed to struggle into a crouched position and, clenching a supporting beam, stood atop the railing. Headlights turned into view a little over a quarter mile away, and every muscle in my body tensed. The chances of dying from a three story fall onto concrete were moderate but if I was also hit by a car...maybe.

"I can't do it anymore," I whispered under my breath. With the headlights quickly approaching, I took slow, deep breaths. "Now or never."

I shut my eyes tightly and let go.

I landed back on the bridge with a thud that reverberated through my spine. I rolled to the side, unable to rise. My whole body shook with sobs, too dehydrated to produce any tears. I stared up at the wisps of clouds racing past the stars.

"Please. I can't." I whispered. I let my drooping eyelids close and waited to stop feeling anything.

112.6 lbs

The walls were devoid of any life or color, much like the patients. We would exchange uncomfortable flitting glances as the therapist attempted to start a word game. Every meal here was much the same; slow, unwilling participation in whatever activity our supervisor thought might distract us from ourselves. It was easy to tell who was new. Old pros would hurriedly gulp down their feast, keenly aware that any hesitation could strip them of their privileges, and us fools who'd just been allowed to join group meals sat staring dejectedly at our food. Even if I had any desire to eat, the rubber hose snaking its way down my throat made swallowing awkward.

I picked at the edges of the tape holding the feeding tube against my face, and craned my neck to peer out a window overlooking the hospital courtyard. Snow fell in sheets covering a smoking nurse in a frigid blanket of white spots. The thick snowflakes nearly obscured the view but at the other end of the hospital I could make out a small girl, bundled in pink being wheeled to a minivan, trying to catch little white slivers on her tongue.

"James?"

"Mmmhmm," I muttered, turning back to the table.

"What's your goal?" the therapist prodded.

"Uh, goal. For here or...like, real life?"

"Up to you."

Half the patients fixed their eyes on me, the others too entranced by their routine to look up. I searched for a cheerful memory that didn't involve calories or weight but everything felt dull in comparison. Becoming a choreographer had always been the future I'd clung to but it seemed melancholic now. Every tangible livelihood I'd pieced together in daydreams turned sour in my mouth.

"I um, I don't know." I brought my hand to the base of my throat, my thumb tracing a circle around my tiny Adam's apple. I remembered curling up in my mother's lap, my head resting on her shoulder, breathing in her perfume as she read aloud Harry Potter novels. She'd squeeze my hand and trace a circle in my palm. "I guess, I want to enjoy things again or... feel alive at least. And maybe..."

I tried to remember the last time I'd even touched another human being in a loving way. It had been nearly three months since Alex and I'd collided in the stairwell but it was the most recent thing I could recall. Would it be delusional to think he would ever take me into his arms and trace shapes on my skin? "...I would like to feel close to someone."

"That sounds like a good place to start," she replied. The same prompt continued around the table, and the weight of everyone's stares lifted off my chest. The girl next to me seemed to have the same amount of trouble coming up with an answer. At least I wasn't alone.

A good place to start. Where was I supposed to start? I let my gaze fall to the tray in front of me. Oh. I pressed my hand against my collar and sighed. I could feel alive if I just let myself. *Even if you eat, you'll never be happy.* Shut up.

The solution was right there, tangible and real; more substantial than any nagging presence. There would be no way to reach the finish if I never made it past the starting line.

Slowly, shakingly, I took the first bite.

Between Your God and Mine
By Sean William Dever

Our love exists – nestled between the stained soil of Palestine
and the deserted farmlands in eastern Galway.

In Suras etched on your tongue
and gold crosses laid around my neck.

If tradition and culture could speak
I wonder if they'd consider the years.

We take pictures and print them out
to compile an archive

as evidence to plead our case. Photos
of apple-picking in New Hampshire,

ER visits at Mass General, and three
consecutive years revisiting the photo booth

where our eyes were trained on one another –
all these danced fearless in the eyes of scripture

and smiled with defiance. I wonder
if I were to remove my bones, lay them around our apartment,

truly build a home for us out of all that I have,
if we can then say this is valid, this is legitimate.

If I meet God before our vows
are etched into my skin, I will ask

what more could we have done.

there are raccoon kits behind my bedpost wall, and I begin to question my fertility
By Sean William Dever

like the tinnitus evanescent in my ears their claws scratch
against the drywall come morning when mother leaves.

I press my hand vertically along the egg-cream paint and
wait for them to feel the warmth emitted; a foreign sun.

And although work and the signs of a failed infusion set attempts
to pull me from my bed I try my best to coo, to purr, to chirp;

allow them to feel safe. Safe in a new body, in a new home,
amongst sounds and scents alien to those of nature.
`
I place my left hand with my right, try my best
to be a heater of sorts, at least until their mother returns

so that they may rest until nightfall. Yet the buzzing of my tech
blisters my ears and as I look down blood is being birthed

along my abdomen. But mother raccoon hasn't returned yet
and I don't want her babies to cry, so I wrap my blanket

around my stomach and return my hands before they wake.
When she scurries up the drainpipe running, to my window,

and she creeps into the attic, lowers herself down into their nest,
into the home within a home she has made for her children.

And I remain vigilant, knowing that I the gift of life and children
is one that may escape the rigid outlines of my body; that the hollow

outlines within myself may erase with wear; that tech may fail;
but that these hands will not as long as I can still be a source

for something else to depend on.

A Thousand Paper-Cuts
By Scott Wheatley

I've witnessed the passing away of memories.
Thoughts of good old times
have been burned and controlled by a sovereign puppet
with the back of the hand.
       And the hand let's go.

The lonely balloon clinging effortlessly
to a naked branch as the bitter wind blows,
and winter's howl closes in.
       And the hand twists the wrist.

We are all crushed under these circumstances.
The blade, the barrel, the bullet.
       And the hand is plastered with paper-cuts.

Red Sky Morning

By Scott Wheatley

The dull edges of the world
Seem smudged by time and adrenaline
This is where I've lived.
Where I will live. Quid pro quo: Fix mine and I might fix yours.

They're ripping my house apart.
This infinite flow; something sticky isolated from the past.
If I had ever lived it.
Like it's locked away,
Buried with your impoverished soul
Waiting for another time
When all is calm

Blame This on the Misfortune of Your Birth
By Sheena Carroll

I doubt you'll ever read this. After all, you were the one who abandoned Chicago. The one who said that you loved neurotic girls, but not enough to stop beating the shit out of the one you tricked into moving to Buffalo with you. But maybe you will.

In that case, hello. This is a brief log of a series of events. The location: Wicker Park - specifically, a café in Wicker Park. But I won't be too specific because I don't want you to recognize it if you ever do come here. I want you to walk past every coffee shop in this damn neighborhood, not knowing if I will be sitting in a seat by the window. Staring at you. Smiling.

The current season is spring, though in Chicago it can better be considered as Winter, Part II. But this is a bizarre March day, and man, bizarre is beautiful. The massive front windows of the shops and bars are open wide; passersby could place out a hand and grab my coffee as we speak. But they won't, because I'd throw my laptop at them. I tell them this with my eyes.

I am between shifts at my between-jobs job. I am writing. I should be working on that ghostwriting project, but I'll save that for tonight. I'm doing great.

I think it is high time that I come to terms with what you did. And with what I did, but mostly what you did. I will never forgive you. I will never forget. And I will never let you forget, either.

I love Chicago, but I don't write about it much. This may be the first time I have since I moved here – fantasy becoming reality, fiction becoming truth, all that good stuff. It's hard to write about Chicago because I get embarrassed; after living here for a while, I realized that everything I'd written about it in the past was grossly inaccurate.

I don't write about Buffalo, either. There's nothing to write about except how cold and wet it is, and how I spent my whole time living there without waterproof shoes because I am both poor and not good at planning ahead. I wore four-year old Crocs on the day of the move. I was asking for my ankles to be broken. *Asking for it.*

As I write this, I realize that I don't want to talk about Chicago or Buffalo anymore. If you want to know what it's like, experience it yourself. You've already experienced Buffalo; I now envision you there, wrapped up in warm blankets and drinking tea in some sort of blue collar hygge ritual. If you experience Chicago, you will regret it. Because I am everywhere here: the bitter lake effect winds that make your eyes water? Me. The leering man getting too close to you at the Blue Line stop? Me. Each and every single brat on the Navy Pier is also me, and if you get too close, they/we will throw their/our ice cream on you.

I don't want to talk about you either, so I'm not. Instead, I am addressing you. This is a threat and should be perceived as such.

I look out the café window. Something in the air smells amazing. I think it's fresh-baked bread.

My phone keeps vibrating, but it's not time to go back to work yet and I am afraid that I'm being asked to come in early. *Afraid.* What a fun word. It describes how I feel about you, but it also describes you. You are so afraid that you had to make me feel afraid to feel a bit better. I think you should see a therapist, and my therapist agrees.

This is a log of a series of events. These events are mundane but safe. These events make me happier than I've been in years. I am alone, all alone in the biggest city I've ever lived in. I get lost here often. Being lost and alone isn't that bad, at least from my perspective.

I hope that being lost and alone makes you very, very *afraid*.

sister milkshake diner
By Taylor Pannell

except something underneath the uttermost below
near things under which I used to say about
nearly any thought most thought utterly said
it was frequently, most of what to say not listen,
to things the little girl said, she's just little
emotionally utterly below things which they say
around, over there, I am emotionally still

at huntington beach somethington speech, closed girl circles
Isabelle Izzy speak fizz no Lydia Lidy
over there ladybug lidy little girl, home-school
listen to fizzabelle most of what to say, listen
somethington going to circle, party huntington speech
things only happen at cash county speech county
utterly exchange something to say not listen
home-stay lydia lidybug exchange nothing

stay at home, basement county little girl
huntington speech is closed no beach here is closed
diner at the end of the pier is where to stay lidy girl
keep your basement, closed by listening beach
listens to your speech, you know what to say
in milkshake diners circled by my waves
around, in the basement where our diners both
utterly exchange the same waves

sonnet to the one that's driving
By Taylor Pannell

thank you, I'm so quiet but sure I'm a-
live or I sense you have seen me holding
my eyes you are pale with stage presence under contrast, you know? (arms out) no feeling?
passion is like a yellow road sign in

the night. too drunk with all prolific-ness
It wasn't about you couldn't have been
all distraction, I'm sorry to just sit
thank you for being here. lip-syncing go
ahead, broken traffic light, I know this
street or stanza full with blackout windows
look around (try to) outside the present

you're welcome, connecting the white lines
car headlights face me, fix this old lie

The Afterlife is a Dining Car
By Theresa Hamman

Prepare yourself,
the light says,
a train comes.

I stand in the middle of the track.

The sky, in all its dreadful beauty,
Fills up with steam,
dust, papers in the train's wake.

Against daybreak the whistle blows.

Here it comes.

Is there really some great god
that will magic me up
in the gasp before impact and spirit
me into the dining car
where a last supper is all prepared
and waiting for me, where
the Holy Grail holds
the long lost elixir of everlasting life?
And I can drink my fill?

I believe fullness is my future.

But the brief millisecond between
breath and death is no sigh into the afterlife.

Here it comes.

Should I leap away?
Can I leap away?

I ask the light.

Prepare yourself,

-/-

passengers
feast on
candied apples,
honey hams,
lobster, duck a l'orange
with sugar snap peas,

bird-beaked children,

peck at grapes, cherries, spit
pits onto the plate

of an ancient woman, whose
hair holds moth balls, she
picks her teeth
with a knife.

-/-

The light assures me
You are not dead,
but awake
in a field
somewhere in Ohio, your bed
moved there years ago

The train slows
and I see a hill rolling
over a field of bluebells and
a maple holding the four poster,
complete with a robin's nest

the eggs gone.

The train stops, a crow
lights on my head, drops
into my hand
a ticket, with words—

No expiration date

embossed in golden script.

I step down, look
at the tree bed, *how*
am I going to get up there?

the light answers,
fly.

A Boy and His Dog
By Tyler Nichols

A scream of terror bounced along the walls of the bunker. Then another. Before long the screams grew more and more intense. Then nothing. Eerie silence overtook the halls. Then footsteps.

"Come on. Work. Work!" a man in a lab coat said as he hobbled along the hallway. He favored his left leg, which dragged along the concrete floor, leaving a crimson trail in its wake. He smacked a flashlight against his palm—the universal sign for trying to power it on.

"Why the hell won't you work?" he screamed at it, as if it'd respond.

An inhuman screech resonated from the hallway behind him and his eyes widened in terror. It was already too late. Something yanked on his ankle and, before he could scream in response, he disappeared into the darkness, scratching and clawing at the floor as he went.

A light flickered. Then *ZAP!*

The man emerged from the darkness with an even more noticeable limp, and fresh blood coating one side of his body. He ran as fast as his legs would carry him. His momentum took him too far, his body slamming into the sealed door at the hallway's end. He plucked away at the keycode, trying to input the correct series of numbers but repeatedly failing. He couldn't focus. His world had become more and more of a blur and all he could feel was the throbbing pain all along the right side of his body.

He turned his head back towards the darkness, his eyes scanning for any form of movement.

Then a massive explosion ripped through the building, flames rising in the back room. The lights flickered again, for a brief moment turning on, before the sprinklers rained water from the ceiling. The light returned but this time, a flashing red hue as the PA system screeched: "Warning! Fire! Warn—"

Footsteps resonated from down the hall.

The man could feel the goosebumps on his neck as each bubbled to the surface. The lights flashed off for a second and all he could hear was the water mixed with his own heavy breathing. When the red glow returned, the man could finally see it: the serrated teeth peering out behind its near-smiling maw.

He quickly turned back to the keycode and tried it one last time. It rang out it's tone of acceptance and he pushed the door open, the orange glow of the sun giving him a moment of hope.

Only a moment.

The teeth appeared from the doorway and closed down around the man's head in an instant; well before any amount of life could muster a flash before his eyes.

The headless body dropped to the ground, rolling slightly down a hill, into the treeline. Its skull remained in the creature's mouth. It snarled before ingesting the flesh and bone in one giant gulp. Its snout lifted into the air and in one swift motion, darted to the forest, honing in on the rest of its meal.

§

Danny stomped down his driveway, book bag slung around his shoulder, and a scowl adorned his bruised face. As he grew closer to his house, he noticed the Pontiac Sunfire with shitty decals sitting in what was usually his father's spot. He rolled his eyes and detoured his route to walk by alongside the vehicle. He gave it a good kick—clearly not thinking it through enough as his toes smashed together against the tire.

"Motherfu-"

The bushes rustled in the tree line, well beyond the car. Danny perked up, eyes going back and forth along the bushes and trees but seeing nothing.

"I told you not to do that, my dad has a nose like a dog." Danny heard his sister say from the house and rage boiled up inside of him.

Danny slammed the front door, hoping to alert the entire house. He turned towards the living room, scowl equipped, but the room was empty. He sighed. Of course, they were in *her* room.

He continued his stomping frenzy all the way up the stairs.

"I hope you jump off a bridge, don't make it all the way, smack against the side, skip down to the water and a shark eats your face off," Danny yelled at his sister, throwing his bookbag at her bedroom door which quickly opened up in response. His older sister stood, fuming in the doorway. "And he'll just eat your face, so you'll still just float in the ocean, waiting to drown. But with no face." He was proud of this one.

"Are you kidding me, you little spaz?" Frankie yelled right back. Danny could see her boyfriend, Terrance, sitting on the bed behind her, a pipe in hand. He hardly seemed interested in intervening. All attention was on the mighty pipe.

"You left me. All the buses were gone and I had to walk. You know how long that is?"

"Mile and a half. Walked it plenty. Quit being a baby."

"Something could have happened to me!" Danny reasoned.

"Oh yeah? Was the football team being mean to you?" she feigned caring, glancing back at Terrance to make sure he hadn't magically evaporated. That's when she noticed the bruise on his face and her expression switched to one of concern. "What happened? Was it those two little shits?"

Was she actually showing a moment of legitimate compassion—

"Fuckers probably were trying to get back at me for throwing that giant tube of lube at 'em. Tracy was sooo mad." She turned to her boyfriend, "Remember that, babe?"

Unbelievable.

"That's right, be your usual bitchy self. You're only my sister when it's actually convenient for you." He had all night to spit facts at her. He had been practicing the entire walk home.

"Babe," came a voice from behind her and suddenly, time was up.

Frankie looked back at her sweetheart, then back to her brother, "Grow the fuck up."

"Enjoy getting VD you—"

She slammed the door in his face. He finished in a whisper, "...fucking skanky...whore..bag."

He wasn't proud as soon as the words left his mouth and was grateful he had only whispered them. Still, he felt betrayed. And hell hath no fury like a 12 year old scorned.

"You're paying for the pizza tonight!" He yelled through the door.

The perfect revenge.

He started walking back towards his room before stopping, sighing, and picking up his backpack in a moment of defeat.

Danny plopped down into his computer chair and started up his PC. He twirled a nearby fidget spinner as it booted. He liked how it helped him deal with his anger, as stupid as it looked. By the time his start screen was loaded, he had already clicked the "Steam" icon and waited for it to expand. It did, almost as fast as his trial notification for Norton Anti-Virus, and he was off to his gaming library.

He started up one, played for a few minutes, then shut it down. Starting up another game, he repeated this process five or six times before he finally gave up. He did a quick refresh of his friends list which still read "0 Friends Online" and sighed in annoyance.

Almost on cue, a voice pierced through from the other side of the door: "Hey, Danny. If you want Pizza it needs to be picked up at Joe's in 30 minutes."

Danny could barely contain himself. He nearly sprinted to the door and yanked it open, breathing heavily like a rabid beast. He was furious.

"Are you fucking kidding me?"

"Don't swear. You're too young for that shit."

"I'm four years younger than you!" He reasoned. "You swear more than me."

"Yeah well, I'm older and I'm in charge, so Mom will listen to me when I tell her you wouldn't stop cursing."

"Go suck yourself."

"Go...suck—okay I'm not dealing with this. Go get the pizza and I won't tell Mom that her son is a weird little pervert." She pulled a wad of cash from her jean jacket vest and forced it into Danny's hand.

"Fine. But I'm getting cinna-twirls. And I'm eating them all before I get back."

"There's already an extra order of them." She winked at him and retreated back to her room before he could even protest. She had a way of doing that.

In fact, he was already halfway out the door again before he even remembered he was supposed to be mad.

Not that it mattered.

Pizza.

Danny was out on the road in a flash. His bike tires hadn't been filled since the prior Spring and he had no way of doing it himself. But thankfully he had a nifty pair of rollerblades.

He glided down the street in them, feeling almost majestic as the wind brushed against his face.

The pizza place was exactly one and a half miles away, and Danny knew he could make it there in fifteen minutes. The way back would prove a little more difficult, but he'd already decided on taking a little break and enjoying a slice to himself before bringing it back to his dumb sibling and her loser boyfriend.

He was busy fantasizing about the mouth-watering pizza when he noticed a rustling in the bushes on the far side of the road. He skidded to a halt and searched with his eyes around the area. His mom always warned him about coyotes, but he'd never seen one. Frankie said he couldn't because they were so fast and that they'd be gone before he even noticed them.

Well he just saw *something* and he refused to not follow through. This was his chance.

Stepping off the pavement, roller blades and all, he felt a sense of pride. The pizza would be there forever, but the chance to see a coyote? That was only a small window.

"God dammit," he said as he spotted the culprit.

It was just a squirrel.

Then a giant set of teeth lunged from the darkness and took down the squirrel in one bite.

Danny's jaw dropped as he witnessed the carnage.

"You're a big coyote," he said stupidly.

The creature was much bigger than Danny expected. The only thing that really matched up in his mind was that it walked on all fours. Even the teeth were more gruesome than he imagined. And its eyes, yellow slits which didn't budge from its target.

But he'd just eaten. There was no way the thing was hungry. Though it was a big boy...

"Are you a... good boy?" Danny said as comforting as possible. The creature just looked at him.

Then Danny remembered something he'd always been told to do in order to gain a dog's trust: let them smell you.

He extended his hand towards the creature and slowly walked forward. It twitched at the sight of him moving. With another twitch, it cocked its head to the side. He was curious.

"It's okay...girl?" he said, leaning down to try and spot any sign of its gender, but seeing nothing.

The closer Danny got, the more details he started to notice. The dark black pelt had a certain sheen to it that he couldn't quite decipher. Was it wet? Was it...gooey? His eyes followed along its body, down its legs, which were a lot bigger than he'd expected. It wasn't like anything he'd seen befo—claws.

Claws.

Oh my fucking god what are those?!

He stopped. His eyes widened. His mouth dropped.

"Fucking badass, dude!" Danny lost all sense of caution and moved forward in a hurry, like he'd just seen an abandoned twenty-dollar-bill.

The creature did not share his enthusiasm, scooting back, confused. It lowered its head, eyes still trained on Danny.

"You're a good boy."

He patted the creature on its head. It twitched to the side, its head cocked and the sharp maw directly next to Danny's soft wrist.

It sniffed again, still cautious.

Then it jumped forward, burying its heading into Danny's stomach, who fell to the ground, letting out a scream.

Then a giggle.

The creature kept rubbing the top of its head against Danny's stomach, like a playful dog. He scratched behind—what he assumed was its ear— or at least his hearing receptor, and the creature responded with a lift of the leg, and a scratch at the air. Its long tongue exited its mouth, snaking around its own head, up to Danny and scratching him behind the ear. He pushed away the slimy muscle with a smirk, "I'm not sure I need the bath but thanks."

He continued scratching it like a dog, hitting all the spots he would on your average Lassie, and the creature responded in kind.

"What on earth are you?" he said as he pulled away his hand, an oily sheen covering it. Its serrated teeth were unlike any he'd ever seen. It almost looked like that thing from the clown movie Frankie always watched.

Out of nowhere, the creature perked up, alert. His head twitched to the side and he darted away, disappearing into the bushes.

"Wait!" Danny yelled after him. "Don't go!"

Another rustling in the bushes and a coyote hurried towards him, running past Danny and into the treeline. The creature was right behind, disappearing just behind the coyote. Then a yelp.

"Oh no," said Danny, worried about his new friend. He ran in the direction they headed but didn't have to go far.

It emerged from the bushes, a tail hanging from its mouth, slurping up the final part of its meal.

"You are a fucking badass."

The creature let out a giant belch then sniffed frantically at the ground. It returned to the spot where the coyote had emerged but found nothing.

"You hungry boy?"

Its head turned towards Danny in an instant.

"You know that word do you?"

Buzz!

The sudden vibration of Danny's phone sent the creature into defense mode, shifting its weight onto its hind legs, assessing the threat.

"Don't worry, bo—girl?" Danny said, bending down and again trying to inspect further but still having no luck. "Uh, I take it you don't follow those rules."

It tilted its head to one side, looking at Danny curiously. Every word Danny spoke, the creature looked more and more eager. Almost like it was learning with every syllable. Then, out of nowhere, it leaned down and started licking in between its legs like it was trying to find the center of a lolli.

"Boy."

Figuring the call was about to go to voicemail, Danny took at peek to see who exactly was calling and the moment he could even make out Frankie's name, he shoved his phone back into his pocket.

"Let's go get some real food."

Danny rolled into the pizza shop with an aura of confidence he hadn't previously known existed. While he made sure to go in alone, just knowing that he had backup made him feel better. More in charge of the situation. Impervious to—

"How's your eye, D-Bag?" said a voice in the corner that stopped Danny in his tracks.

You've got to be kidding me.

"I think he's still mad about it," another voice said.

Danny looked over at the two bullies he'd had run in's with on multiple occasions: Derek and Lyle. Danny touched the present under his eye that the two had given him earlier in the day. He didn't know what to do. Then he remembered.

"Can't be mad at idiots being idiots. Mom always taught me that."

"What did you say?!" Derek pushed up Danny against the wall, shoving his forearm into his throat.

"Hey! Enough of that! Take it outside, you goddamn hood rats!" the Pizza Shop Owner yelled at them from behind the counter. "I'll call the cops so fast you'll be in jail before Dinner. And take those damn rollerblades off when you're in my store!"

"Just make sure the pizza is ready when I come back in," said Danny with so much confidence that Derek and Lyle exchanged a look of bewilderment. They nodded their heads at each other and smacked their fists together, following Danny outside.

As they exited the Pizza Place, they just barely caught the back of Danny disappearing around the corner.

"You can't get away from us, you pussy!" Derek shouted.

"Gonna regret that mouth of yours, you little bitch," Lyle growled, rounding the corner of the building.

"So wait," stood at the end of the alley, "Am I pussy or a bitch?"

"You're whatever the fuck we call you!" Derek said, making his way towards Danny. They still had most of the alley to traverse, but Danny still stood his ground, unflummoxed.

"Funny you say that." He looked at Derek. "Because I'm gonna call you Pussy." He looked at Lyle. "And you Little Bitch." Danny's grin was so wide that he could only imagine how much it was infuriating them. But it only made him smile wider.

"You're not gonna be smiling when I punch your teeth through your ass—"

Buzz!

Danny's phone went off and the bullies paused, not wanting to have the wraith of a parent brought down upon them. But Danny knew it wasn't a parent even before he checked the caller ID.

He answered, annoyed. "What do you want, Frankie?"

"Where the hell are you? You've been gone for-fucking-ever."

"I got held up. Just... dealing with something."

"Terrance and I are hungry so what ever you're doing, deal with it."

"Okay, Frankie," he said as he stared at the bullies with pure venom. "We'll deal with it."

A smile spread across his face.

The clock struck 7:00, and Frankie tapped her foot impatiently against the kitchen floor.

"I'm gonna fucking kill him," said Frankie, fuming.

"It's not a big deal. He'll get here eventually. I just hope he didn't forget breadsticks," Terrance said while he fiddled with his phone.

"Doesn't mean murder isn't justified,"

Terrance stopped for a moment, going back and forth on Frankie's double negatives before raising his eyebrows and returning to his phone.

"Sorry I'm late."

Frankie and Terrance's attention turns towards the door where Danny now stood, covered head to toe in blood and barefoot.

"Oh my god what happened?"

Frankie ran up to Danny, grabbing onto him and looking for the wound that had produced so much blood.

"Terrance, call the police."

"No, I'm fine," Danny protested yet still just stared forward, refusing to make eye contact with Frankie.

"You're fine?!" Frankie could hardly contain herself. "No, you are not fucking fine. What's the matter with you? Stub your toe and you cry for hours and now you're cool as a fucking cucumber?"

"Terrance, can you go check my bike?"

"Yeah, Danny. No problem." Terrance was out the door, wanting to be useful.

"Danny, you have to tell me what happened," Frankie pleaded.

"I told you I'm fine."

"You're covered in blood! What the fuck do you mean? You're in shock."

"Frankie, it's not mine."

"What?"

Danny finally turned his head to face Frankie, staring into her eyes.

"It's not my blood."

A scream of terror erupted outside.

"Terrance!" Frankie rose from next to Danny and was running to the door when he said calmly, "I wouldn't go out there if I were you."

She stopped, heeding his warning.

The screaming had subsided. Whatever had happened, it was over now.

"Remember when we were little and Grandma and Grandpa used to take us to the park with the big wooden pirate ship? You and I would run around until we didn't have any energy whatsoever. Then we'd go back to them, get stocked up on Mountain Dew, and we'd be off again. Went from playing Tag to Hide and Go Seek to Stay The Fuck Away From Me. Remember that? I was your brother yet all you cared about was yourself. Didn't want to hang out with the little kid anymore. And no matter how many people told you to be there for me, you never were. Every time I needed you, you pretended I didn't exist. I mean hell, today all I needed was a ride. A simple ride home and this wouldn't have happened." He raised a finger and rested it upon his bruised cheek.

"It's always extremes with you. When I walked through the door, you weren't worried about me. You were worried about what Mom would do to you. Well, Frankie. Mom's not here. And now you have to worry about what I'm going to do to you."

"What did you do to Terrance?" her lips quivered as she spoke.

"Me? I didn't do anything to Terrance." There's a rustling on the front stoop. "But there's someone I want you to meet." Danny reached back and pushed open the screen door.

"Oh my god."

One claw at a time, the creature entered the house, its snarling teeth dripping in blood. Frankie stared at it in terror, putting everything together.

"You're a fucking psychopath."

"No, Frankie. I'm just a boy. And this is my dog. Don't worry. He just wants to play."

Outside, the screams erupting from the house were nearly drowned out in the night wind. No, not wind.

Helicopters.

Far above the house, in the night sky three copters closed in on the property. A man leaned out the side of one of the helicopters and examined the carnage below. Raising a walkie to his mouth, he shouted, "We've found the creature. Take it alive. Kill the bo—"

The front door of the house opened and the boy walked out, followed closely by the creature. The man watched intensely as the boy pointed to something, and the creature responded, grabbing it.

The man's eyes opened wide and he smiled. "Take them both alive."